Praise for Jorrie Spencer's
Anchor

"The characters in the story are all well drawn. The author gives the wolf pack a mythology and a background that makes reader's care about what is happening."

~ *RT Book Reviews*

"What makes *Anchor* work very well is the swift-paced taut and engaging narrative. From page one to last, I am at the edge of my seat wanting to find out what happens next."

~ *Mrs. Giggles*

"...this shifter story is captivating, sexy, dangerous and exciting."

~ *Long and Short Reviews*

"I really enjoyed the overall world building Spencer created for this book. The magical abilities of Mala's was something I'd never seen done before in any other book, and I loved the way it was woven through the story line..."

~ *The Book Pushers*

Look for these titles by
Jorrie Spencer

Now Available:

Haven
Selkie Island

Northern Shifters Series
The Strength of the Pack
The Strength of the Wolf
Puma
Anchor

Anchor

Jorrie Spencer

SAMHAIN
PUBLISHING

Samhain Publishing, Ltd.
11821 Mason Montgomery Road, 4B
Cincinnati, OH 45249
www.samhainpublishing.com

Anchor
Copyright © 2012 by Jorrie Spencer
Print ISBN: 978-1-60928-435-0
Digital ISBN: 978-1-60928-427-5

Editing by Sasha Knight
Cover by Angela Waters

First Samhain Publishing, Ltd. electronic publication: April 2011
First Samhain Publishing, Ltd. print publication: March 2012

Dedication

To my family.

Prologue

Caleb ran. His muscles burned. His heart beat the rapid tattoo of death—the too-fast rhythm that presaged blacking-out terror. He couldn't face that pain again so he pushed himself harder, not caring that his efforts were futile.

Mala could sense all this. Of course she could. After all, Caleb was the latest of a long string of terrified wolves to star in her dreams.

The forest through which he ran was dark, damp. Winter hadn't quite ended and freezing temperatures made the paths tricky to navigate, dangerous. He could fall and it would be all over.

In her nightmare, Caleb feared his father was going to kill him. That this time, he wasn't going to heal from a mauling—for wolves, or werewolves in Mala's dreams, could shift and fix themselves.

Caleb's fear was compelling and drew Mala to him, and as his fear grew, so did her anger—it wasn't what anyone should have to endure. Especially in *her* nightmare. She was determined to control those.

The reality of her dream unnerved her. She literally felt Caleb take a corner too sharply, his hind legs fly out from under him, and it lost him precious time, scrambling to recover from his almost-fall. His father closed in.

She had to ask, to make some sense of her latest night terror. *"Why is your father chasing you?"*

But Caleb didn't know. He wondered why his father tortured him. He was fifteen, almost sixteen, and he'd thought the beatings would end when he grew up. Yet here he was, being hunted.

"Hunted?" A kind of dismay grew within Mala. She hated the violence of it all. But he ignored her question so she took another tack.

"You call yourself Caleb." A statement this time.

"Of course I call myself Caleb." The fear flowed through him, turned bright as it met and melded with Mala's anger. Anger that this was happening again. That the creatures in her dreams could be so battered by their dream lives.

His paws scrabbled, like his mind, trying to find purchase on slippery ground, on mud turned to ice. His confused emotions became her focus—he didn't understand how she could be inside him.

"Yes," she thought at Caleb. *"I am here, anchored in you."* Those words meant little to him but nevertheless determination filled her, and she let that determination flow towards him. *"Now, Caleb, hand over your fear to me."*

The release was simple, he was too scared to do anything else but give his fear to her. She pulled the emotion out of him, this strange capacity she had while dreaming, of creating weapons from emotions.

She gave him time to calm down as she did her work, building the blade that would take down Caleb's pursuer, free both the wolf in her dreams and herself from the monster. As the father gained ground and Mala gained power, she prepared to take the next step, though it would shock the young wolf.

"Caleb, I'm ready." She let him absorb this before giving the

instruction. *"Slow down."*

"What? No!*"* Some of the fear she'd taken from Caleb rebounded as his body opened like a wound drawing in poison. Her focus intensified, refocused, until she was once again drawing his fear out, refashioning the bright weapon ever stronger.

"Weapon?" he asked, dimly aware of what she was doing and thinking. They were part of each other now, and their thoughts and emotions bled into one another.

"Trust me. I am your only hope." For she had seen this happen too many times before to do anything but stand and confront the monster. There was no longer the possibility of escape without her fighting, and the idea of Caleb being destroyed hurt too much.

Despair filled Caleb in knowing she was his only hope. He didn't understand that in her dream she was powerful. But she could use his despair, too, and pulled it towards her to bind the fear and make it sharper, more deadly.

"Let me do this, Caleb. Slow down, turn around and face your father."

"He'll kill me." His anguish caused her to flinch. Yet she took the anguish as well, hardening that blade of fear and despair, as his father came closer. The end was near.

"Caleb," she thought calmly. *"Please trust me. Face him."*

He didn't want to.

She sent out a wave of reassurance, threaded it with hope, and felt it roll through him. *"You must understand, I can fight him. This is my world. Turn now."*

She felt Caleb's chest hollow out with hopelessness, but he did as she asked, slowing then wheeling around to face his pursuer. He could barely catch his breath as his shaking wolf body went low to the ground in submission, and his ears flattened, asking his father for mercy when she knew none was to be found.

"That's it." She let her satisfaction pulse through him. *"Your father will never know what hit him."*

Caleb found this idea bizarre, that his father was no match for her. But she watched his father through his gaze. The larger, older wolf, golden-eyed, brown-furred, came to a stop.

The father was gloating, which didn't surprise Caleb. The monster-wolf always gloated before meting out punishment. The son sometimes thought it was his father's perfect moment, the anticipation unbearably pleasurable.

"Asshole," she decided, and despite all his doubts, that description of his father buoyed Caleb.

The weapon she had fashioned, a substance like white light—sharp and strong with fear—she let Caleb see it briefly. After all, some of its substance was his. She always found her weapons strangely beautiful, a white beyond whiteness that couldn't be described outside of her dream. And this one shone.

"Goodbye, Caleb. Remember this—when I leave you, you must run."

She could feel his confusion but had no time to explain.

"Watch," she told him with a kind of pride as she faced forward and flung herself like a weapon, an arc of movement through the ether of her dream. With the blade she'd fashioned, she sliced through air and deep into his father, the sharp brightness wrought from Caleb's fear and confusion, and her own anger.

She aimed for the monster's heart, cut into it, then held still.

There was always this moment, as the heart pulsed around

her, where she feared she might fail. And this one's heart was strong, fighting her.

She held on until, under her influence, the heart slowed its beat and gradually stilled.

For long seconds, the wolf, the monster-father, stood tall, even with his silent heart. She could sense his tension as he strove against an alien presence that hid itself within him. It was with relief that Mala experienced his body drop to the ground. There was the slightest bounce and then no movement at all.

As if from a great distant came the sound of a whine—Caleb's. She couldn't see the young wolf, for his father's eyes had closed and she remained focused inwards. But she could feel Caleb's presence, sense his trembling approach.

With all she had in her, she held his father's heart motionless while she thought at Caleb with as much power as possible, *"Run, Caleb, run again."*

He needed no further encouragement. One moment he was there, stunned by this unfathomable development, the next he was gone. A lack of presence and she waited alone, feeling grim.

It was a dream, she reminded herself, beginning to shake from the exertion of holding the monster-wolf still. *Only a dream*—where she had strange and unusual powers and rescued terrified wolf creatures. None of it made sense, but that was the way of dreams after all. It had taken her a lifetime to learn how to save the vulnerable ones.

And yet, in the end, she finished this by fleeing for she refused to become ensnared. She had to rise out of the darkness that threatened to become a trap and make her way home.

How long could dream wolves stay dead before they didn't recover from their injuries?

"From what I see, there's a skinny, underfed, underage wolf who can't decide what to do and doesn't know he's being watched." The strange young wolf could be a female, Angus knew, but males outnumbered females on a scale of about twenty-five to one so it was less likely. Jancis's voice dropped. "He's making me sad. I'm a bit worried he's going to collapse from starvation to be honest."

Crap, more than underfed. "Where?"

"East side. I can see him from the video feed attached to the barn. He goes into it, gets uncomfortable and leaves before he can manage to grab something to eat. He can't settle. Not the actions of a wild wolf, I don't think."

"I'm on it. Send Rory as backup, but he's only to approach on my say-so." Frightened wolves did better if they weren't outnumbered. On the other hand, Angus wanted someone to help him pin this one down if he was feral. An unfortunate likelihood. He closed the phone and turned back to the woman standing in front of him.

"Eden, I've got to go."

"Is something wrong?" She wasn't always comfortable around people, but nevertheless she worried about them.

"Don't know yet." Angus was constitutionally incapable of lying to his people or he would have said no.

The worry line of her frown deepened, and she gave him a sharp nod as he left.

He ran back to his house, taking all of two minutes, slammed inside and stripped off his clothes. More painful to shift this way, without the full moon calling to his blood and with the sun blazing down outside, but he pulled back his human skin. That's how he thought of it, though every werewolf's mental approach to the shift was different. His wolf felt his urgency and surged to the surface. His skin prickled as if retracting. And there it was, the event horizon. He dropped to his hands and knees, let his shift overtake him as the world grayed out.

You didn't become alpha without decent control and memory, so the confusion that assailed him as he woke from the change—wolf at midday, inside his house, new moon in the sky—was brief. His daughter had phoned him. A starving and possibly feral wolf was hanging around the barn. Angus rose, shook out his body and trotted to his front door. Like every other house in Wolf Town, this had a lever handle, and he pushed down on it with his paw. Jancis would come by to shut it once Angus showed up on the screen.

He loped to the east end of town.

It wasn't complicated, though Angus made a point of approaching from downwind so his scent didn't frighten off the newcomer. He saw the young black wolf tentatively approach the barn. From his size, this one was a teenager, and he worried about them the most. It was an easy age to lose your way, but this pup was seeking help. Angus knew the lure of the barn— shelter from the wind and some tasteless if nutritional jerky in packaging that could be torn open with wolf teeth.

Angus also understood the youth would fear becoming trapped inside the building by a stranger—which was exactly what Angus had planned. He had only good intentions. The trick was convincing the young wolf of that.

He moved silently, reaching the door before he stopped to observe the distracted stranger tearing into some food and gulping it down. Angus let him finish the large swallow before he gave a soft woof.

The youth spun around, body going tight and trembling as he cringed. After a pause—probably assessing if he could get past Angus at the wide door—he dropped to his belly, ears going back, and whined.

That's it, thought Angus, *don't try to flee.* Slow and steady, Angus approached. He anticipated fear in this situation, but the boy's was excessive, as if he expected to be executed for trespassing. Angus whined back reassurance and watched the stranger's ears lift slightly in hope.

In other situations, Angus would have crouched down to show he was no threat and was not interested in dominating anyone, but the black wolf's confusion made that pointless. So Angus approached the pup, who remained still and trembling until Angus nuzzled behind his ear and was assailed by whining and feverish licking. He accepted the supplication—as clearly the youth had been around the dominant-submissive pack dynamics that were so common outside of Wolf Town. Angus then retreated and picked up another package of beef jerky from the bin it was kept in, and threw it over. After a moment's hesitation while eyeing Angus carefully, the wolf couldn't resist ripping open the wrapping and gulping down the food.

They repeated the ritual a few more times so the strange wolf wouldn't collapse from lack of food.

The black body kept trembling, if not so violently. Angus had hoped he could lead the boy to his house and they could shift sometime today, but he no longer saw that as a probable outcome. Undergoing a shift in a stranger's house required a certain level of comfort and trust. Time and patience were needed.

Angus gave an inward sigh. He should have delegated, sent someone else to approach and befriend the boy, because he was going to be out of commission for days on this. Too bad he was crap at delegating. Besides, he wanted this done right for the boy, and he was very good at convincing wolves to trust him.

With a mental shrug, Angus lay down beside the thin wolf to offer him warmth. Though exhausted, the intruder jumped away at that. Angus watched, hoping this wouldn't turn into a chase. He kept his body relaxed, though, while offering another soft woof of encouragement.

C'mon, boy, you're not capable of escaping me, you must recognize that.

And he did, for the pup let his head fall in a sign of surrender. He circled around Angus twice before lying down near him. Angus moved over, again offering warmth. It was late winter after all, and this pup was near skeletal. The young wolf's body shuddered before gingerly pressing against Angus's side. Lethargic from his first food in who knows how long, the boy fell asleep.

Well, that was gratifying, his relative lack of resistance to sleeping beside Angus—or it indicated a dangerous level of physical and mental fatigue. Either way, Angus was going to be here a few days. He could do with a rest, he supposed, and everyone told him he worked too hard.

So that afternoon and evening, he allowed himself to doze while he kept guard over the newest member of Wolf Town.

For four nights, Mala didn't sleep. She paced, she read, she watched DVDs—and she called in sick. This was how she'd lost her old job, and she saw all the signs of it happening again. But she knew herself. She needed the week off to recover from the nightmare and the insomnia that followed. Finally on the fifth day after the nightmare—why were her nightmares all about murderous wolves?—exhaustion took over and she slept for twelve hours straight.

The waking wasn't easy, like swimming through thick, difficult water towards the light, but she eventually made it out, back into the real world, and dragged her body off to the bathroom to shower.

She looked at the mirror and saw dark bags under her eyes—no mystery about the cause of that. Sometimes she feared being unable to pull out of those nightmares, being trapped in them forever. There was no way of being reassured it wouldn't happen when she couldn't even talk to anyone about the dreams and the terrors.

And this last time, determined that the boy, Caleb, get away, she'd stayed longer than ever before. It hadn't mattered that it had all been a dream when, as it occurred, it had felt so incredibly real.

At that, a memory stirred from the depths of her latest sleep. It hadn't been dreamless, and she shivered, unable to release her own gaze in the mirror. The too-skinny black wolf she'd saved had re-entered her dreams, briefly, the previous night. It was like that sometimes. After a sleep terror, her mind would return to the same creature. It had been a calm dream, thank God, no need for action—which always took a toll on her and she couldn't afford more days off work. But this time, Caleb had been sleeping in a barn, and someone had been watching over him in a fatherly way. He was safe.

Safe.

Another shiver shook her, but good for once. Even if it was all a figment of her imagination, she desperately wanted that dark, panicked wolf to be safe. She couldn't disengage but she had learned to control the nightmares by attacking the monster—and there was always a monster in these, to accompany the awful fear. Like Caleb's father, intent on violence.

"In. Your. Dream." She spoke to her mirror self, attempting to sound ironic. *Get a grip, Mala. So you have alarming night terrors*—that's what her parents had called them when, as a child, she'd lie in bed keening until shaken awake by her mother. The point was—it was over.

For now.

She'd once talked to her counselor about her violent dreams, and the well-meaning woman had smiled, her manner condescending. The counselor hadn't been impressed by Mala's obsession with wolves either. She'd been more interested in the fact that Mala didn't make friends easily and had a fraught relationship with her father.

Sure those things weren't great, but Mala couldn't manage to convey to this woman that what defined her, what made her what she was today, were the dreams. And the terrors.

After her little unplanned sabbatical, Mala had been back at work for a week, catching up on the paperwork and trying to ignore the resentment of her coworkers. She understood. They thought she was milking her sick days for all they were worth when they each had too much work in the office for too little pay. So she put in a few twelve-hour days, got her share under control, helped a couple of other women, took the fall for a mistake someone else had made, and stayed obliging when the boss was kind of an asshole about, well, most things.

If she was lucky, she wouldn't have another nightmare for months or even a year. It had happened before, a long dry spell. Once she'd had sixteen months of peace and thought her dreams were over and she'd turned normal. She no longer believed that was a possible future for her.

Nevertheless her last dream, when the black wolf slept, was a good omen. She remembered the feel of the fatherly wolf beside him—clearly *not* his father, given the previous nightmare. This new, older wolf had felt *good*. Again she shivered at the memory of safety.

"Okay, Mala?"

Her face flamed at the idea her boss had been watching her. As if she could explain her crazy thoughts to him, or anyone.

"Absolutely fine," she stated with as much self-possession as possible.

"Excellent." He slammed down a pile of files on her desk with more force than necessary. He wasn't violent, just dramatic, but it made her jump. "These are for you."

"Thank you," she said politely and took them, throwing herself into that work so she wouldn't think about her dreams. Late in the evening, she dragged herself home.

When she fell into bed that night, she was exhausted but hopeful. It looked like she wasn't about to lose her job after all. Competent help was hard to find, and she was competent— when not incapacitated. With that not entirely pleasant thought, she started to drift off to sleep. *Good omen*, she reminded herself, as she pushed away the fear of another night terror.

For all the good it did.

It was a type of waking—at least it felt that way—with the flare of fear like a beacon calling to her. A part of her wanted to ignore it. It was too soon and she was too drained, and the last time she'd see him, Caleb had been safe. But the flare was familiar and compelling, it was *hers*, and she couldn't stop herself. She focused.

Her body fell away, and with it, her reluctance. She was dreaming, everywhere and nowhere, with only the boy's fear her anchor. She arrowed in on Caleb, determined to find him, make him safe. And then she was with him.

He didn't know where he was, strangely enough. All he knew was confusion. After a few moments of blindness, she settled in to look for him, used his eyes to see until he could calm down and see for himself. It was then, observing his bare arms, she realized with some shock he wasn't an actual wolf.

She always dreamed wolves, and her surprise reached him.

"I am a wolf," he told her, and the statement settled him, like he was returning to know himself. He took stock of his situation.

He was in a room, the door not shut, the house quiet, and he breathed in, scenting the presence of two others and trying to figure out how to hide from them.

"I know them." With this thought, relief swept through Caleb. He did not have to hide.

She waited, letting him sort through his uncertain knowledge, not understanding how he could lack such basic information.

"These two people, they're not strangers. They're kind to me." His confidence built with these assertions.

The worst of his panic had ebbed but, just in case, Mala began to fashion a weapon. It would be a weak blade, nothing like the one that had felled his father, because the boy carried none of that intense terror she required to make it strong. But a defense of some kind might come in useful.

"No weapon." He hunched at the idea, and straightened again. The next thought was defiant; he expected her to contradict him. *"These are my friends."*

She paused, the shine of her work in her hands, and she recalled that he'd felt safe in that barn.

He remembered too, and with that memory her work became futile. She only ever attacked the monsters, not friends, not kindness. She let the weapon spread thin, then dissolve.

"I'm glad," she told him.

The last of his fear dissipated, a wary hopefulness taking its place, and her heart hurt for him as she sensed his desire to belong here. She looked out through his eyes once more, and he was staring at a beautiful painting. Three wolves were running up a snow-covered hill, the full moon shining down on them. It made him happy to see it, to recognize himself in the picture— not him exactly but creatures like him. She concentrated, wanting to remember this painting, as if it could be a marker of sorts for her. A way to locate this place, if it was a place.

It became critical that she ask.

"Caleb. Where are you?"

He frowned, thinking about the bedroom and the house.

"What city? What town?"

His brow cleared, his confusion now gone, and she could feel him smile just a little. *"Wolf Town."*

She held on to the words, praying she'd recall them once she left this dream. It seemed important.

"I can't stay," she told him.

He nodded once, unsure what to make of both her presence and her leave-taking.

"But you stay, Caleb. Stay with your friends."

Chapter Two

Angus had slept too much this past week. He'd remained with the pup, in wolf form, until he could be coaxed into Angus's house. It took another night to get the black wolf into a bedroom, the one he would be staying in for a while. Once that was done and Angus was able to carve out some time alone, he shifted back to human. When he came to after that shift, there was the feeling of rightness in his bones. He enjoyed being wolf, but unlike some, not for too long, and he always missed human activity. Jancis had gone to sleep so he couldn't chat with her. Instead, Angus read the mail that had piled up in his absence.

Mostly email, and mostly business related. The government liked that he'd started a business up in northern Ontario, but they also liked electronic paperwork. No question about what he'd be spending tomorrow on.

But first he wanted to touch base with Trey Walters and find out if he'd heard any rumors of runaway teenage wolves. Despite being retired from the FBI and from other ghost agencies Angus didn't want to think about, Trey had more contacts in the shifter community than anyone Angus had ever met. He had just typed in a brief greeting when he went still.

The noise was subtle, but there. After a few minutes, he determined the movement was of the two-legged kind, which made Angus smile with something like relief. This pup was not feral, not when he turned human so easily. Angus had prepared himself for having a wolf in the house for any number of days.

He remained seated a bit longer, giving the boy time to compose himself after a shift, as the confusion of a new place in someone so young might be an issue. Then Angus walked down the hall to meet the stranger he'd brought into his home.

At the sight of Angus in his doorway, the boy started. Angus kept his expression calm, his stance relaxed, and observing that, the tension in the teen's body eased.

Scruffy was the first word that came to mind. The beginnings of a beard, not amounting to much of anything as yet, and hair that had been hacked away by God knows what and not recently. He wore the clothes Angus had left in the room, not his, but still too big on the teen. Baggy.

Soft, uncertain brown eyes blinked up at him from the boy's slight frame, and something in Angus melted. No one was taking this wolf from him, unless it was in the young man's best interests.

"Welcome to Wolf Town. I'm Angus." He held out his hand without stepping forward, making the boy come to him.

His newest ward pulled in a breath, as if steeling himself, before he approached Angus to take his hand and shake, all the while eyeing him. Waiting for... Well, Angus didn't want to think about what the boy was waiting for.

His hand was too cold for a werewolf who'd shifted recently. Shifters gave off a huge amount of heat after the change. So he still wasn't eating enough, despite his last week with Angus. Time to remedy that. Jancis had been buying out the store in their absence, knowing they'd be famished by the time they were humans again. Eden had also sent food over once she'd learned of their newest recruit. She had a soft spot for lost adolescents, given the sad fate of her own boy.

"Come on to the kitchen," Angus told him. "You'd better eat something."

His visitor nodded, and Angus turned away and listened while the boy followed him. He opened the fridge and pulled out a number of containers before deciding microwaved meat stew was the best way to supply his ward with immediate heat, energy and protein.

He wouldn't mind some himself.

"Tell me your name."

He knew the boy was scared to speak. It happened sometimes, this idea that staying silent made you unnoticeable in the pack. But he responded to Angus's command and cleared his throat. "Caleb."

A sturdy name and the tone was more confident than Angus had expected. Deeper voiced too. He might be older than the very young teen he looked.

"Well, Caleb, I'm pleased to meet you. I want you to know that you have a place here."

"You're the alpha?"

Angus wasn't crazy over that term, though he used it to describe himself. Taken from real wolf packs, misunderstood, misused by those in power... Okay, now was not the time for *that* rant. "I'm in charge of a number of things around here, yes."

The microwave dinged, and Angus pulled out the steaming bowl and placed it in front of Caleb. Once he had a spoon in hand, he started vacuuming up the stew, and Angus reached for more food to feed him.

After twenty minutes of brisk eating, Caleb slowed and took on the expression of one who'd eaten too much too fast and needed to sleep. But first, Angus had a few questions.

He set his own empty bowl aside and looked across at Caleb, who immediately froze. Angus wondered what he read in his face, for the set of Caleb's shoulders implied he was waiting for the other shoe to drop now that he'd finished eating and drinking.

"Where are you from?" Angus asked.

Caleb blinked rapidly though he didn't cut his gaze away from Angus as he might have expected a small battered wolf to do. Alpha or no, Angus tended to force his way upon people.

"You don't want to answer that?" Angus surmised.

Caleb firmly shook his head.

"All right. Is that because you're protecting someone?"

"Sorta," he prevaricated, then chewed on his lip.

"So you feel it's safer..."

"If no one I know is notified."

"Because?"

The shoulders slumped and Caleb swallowed. While Angus felt a little guilty, he let the silence weigh on his guest until Caleb admitted, "He'll hunt me down again."

Angus straightened. "Hunt? Who hunts you?"

Caleb's eyes shone with angry fear.

"*No one* hunts you while you're here."

"No one can stop him."

Angus smiled and he knew it was ugly. "I like a challenge, Caleb. I'm in charge, and I say I can stop him. So." Angus clasped his hands together and rested his chin on them as he gazed at Caleb, determined to protect this boy. "Who am I challenging?"

The words came out on a hoarse whisper. "My father."

The next day, despite feeling completely drained, Mala dragged herself to work. It hadn't been a nightmare last night, not really. Yes, the beginning of the dream had had all the markers, with its beacon of fear that seemed to draw her into a frightened wolf. Except that had been a teenage boy, not a skinny black wolf, even if he'd carried the same name of Caleb and felt like the same person in a different body.

Well, dreams weren't supposed to be logical, were they?

Hollow comfort, since she always felt, against her better sense, that her dreams were different. That they meant something. Her mother had sneered at her once while Mala tried to explain. *How special do you think you are, darling, that no one else has dreams like you do?*

It had hurt, that sneer, even if from a distance Mala recognized her mother had been trying to steer her away from taking the dreams too seriously. As if that would solve her problems.

Yet, this last dream had been different. There'd been no live wolves, only three in a painting. Could it have been an ordinary dream? She hadn't had to take control of the situation, she hadn't had to defend anyone. The new dream-Caleb had been human and had friends, and once that point became clear, Mala had floated away, her last memory that painting for goodness' sake.

A normal dream, she longed for those. She probably did have them, even if she didn't remember.

It was hard to focus that day, her energy remained sapped and her attention scattered. She must have acted off or sick or something, because late in the workday her boss abruptly sent her home early, and followed that up with a phone call that informed her she was being let go. The gist of it being that erratic behavior, despite some hard work, wasn't going to cut it with *him.*

Numbed by the dream or by imminent unemployment, she simply hung the phone up on its cradle, incapable of arguing back. God knows, she knew about erratic behavior.

She stared blankly into space, and that old question that never quite left her came at her. What was she going to do?

It had happened again. But she would deal. Though each time, as she grew older and the number of jobs she'd been released from increased, it became more and more difficult to find employment.

How ironic that she wanted to sleep, given that sleep brought her to such terrible places. Though she might be safe today, since the dream boy-slash-wolf had been safe. Sure, it was all in her mind, but so what? If he was safe in her mind, sleep might bring her peace tonight.

And tomorrow? Well, she didn't care if she was loopy. She was too far-gone to let it matter anymore. Tomorrow, she was going to investigate the existence of a place called Wolf Town.

Where dream-Caleb lived.

The name of the town was vaguely familiar. But if Wolf Town *was* from subconscious memory, or if it didn't exist, her investigation would do no one any harm.

And if it did exist, she was going to gather the last of her resources and visit the place. She had this idea, and it made her shake inside, that she could meet Caleb and he could explain everything to her.

It wasn't true. She knew that. No one was ever going to explain anything. Not since her father had told her she was too stupid to understand there was reality and there was fantasy, too stupid to identify the line between them.

But her mind was set on this course of action, for better or worse, and she found herself hoping that something was real, somewhere in this town of wolves.

Chapter Three

Angus felt like he had a limpet attached to him. Everywhere he turned, he found Caleb next to him. It wasn't the same as when, years ago, he'd fostered his kids, Jancis and Rory—they'd been five years old and literally liked to hang off him.

But it was the teenaged equivalent, Caleb slouching in the corner or just happening to saunter into the kitchen after Angus.

Of course he could have shaken him off. Caleb had a wariness about him that suggested he'd easily be discouraged from anyone's company. But Angus had no intention whatsoever of doing anything but nurturing this tentative bond between them. He made a point of staying in the house for most of his work over those first few days, so Caleb could get used to normality and the idea he had a guardian who was happy to have him around.

At some point soon, he wanted Caleb in school, but Angus hadn't broached the idea of education quite yet. Nor had he seen evidence that the boy could read. There were magazines and books about, none of which Caleb had picked up. Shapeshifters had a depressing tendency to be completely unschooled because of abuse, neglect or a simple lack of parenting ability.

In this case, Angus would pin it squarely on the terrorizing father. The phone call from Trey came later than expected, but it did yield results.

As usual, Trey got right down to business.

"The father is John Davies. He came up through the Midwest to the greater wilds of Canada after some violence involving humans. I'd heard of him in my day, but not often. He was careful and his family small in number, when he got along with them. Antisocial for a wolf." The irony in Trey's voice didn't escape Angus. Trey himself was antisocial for a wolf, yet had somehow been installed as the de facto leader of Ontario werewolves. Not only that, after years of solitude he lived with a lynx shifter these days.

Clearly antisocial wolves weren't all the same in quality of character.

Angus was far from antisocial, and they were utterly different, he and Trey, yet Angus had few werewolves he got along with better.

"So no greater ties to a pack or a rogue group of wolves?" Angus asked.

"Not that I know of." In that answer, Angus could almost hear Trey shrug. "Could be stuff under my radar. God knows there always is."

And that was about it. Trey hung up after informing Angus he'd contact him if he heard more.

Next up was a conversation Angus didn't particularly look forward to, but he needed some answers and young Caleb was the only source.

He waited until Jancis went off to work that morning. Caleb was polite to Jancis, even grateful, given that she'd fixed him food and bought him clothes, but she made him anxious in a way Angus didn't. No doubt because Angus had spent a week as wolf with Caleb. The boy needed time.

"Caleb." The boy's gaze cut to him and Angus was pleased to see more eagerness than fear. Either he was very resilient or there'd been a positive force in Caleb's life to counter his father's presence. "I'd like to ask you some questions."

The eagerness faded to sullen guardedness. But sullen felt normal for that age, and Angus was happy enough to see it. He remembered teenaged Jancis and her desire to keep all her secrets from him, despite his being adamant she wasn't going to sneak off at night to have sex with her twenty-year-old boyfriend.

"Okay," Caleb finally allowed.

"Who is your mother?"

He looked surprised, and he'd probably been bracing himself for a question about his father. He opened his mouth and closed it again.

"You want to protect her?"

Caleb nodded.

"From your father, or someone else?"

"My dad. Though he has friends who...help him."

"I'm not going to give your mother away, Caleb."

Caleb swallowed, accepting that. "Her name's Shanna. She lives in Chicago, but my father doesn't know that. I don't think."

"Okay," Angus said encouragingly.

"It's the one way she can escape him, living in a big city, but I couldn't stay there anymore."

Teen wolves especially needed places to run. Chicago didn't supply much of that type of wilderness.

"So she arranged for me to stay at a few different places. But somehow my dad always found me."

"What happened the last time your dad found you?"

Caleb let out a long, shaky breath and his gaze sheered away. He wasn't submissive, that's for sure. He liked to look Angus in the eye, not necessarily challenging, and the openness there gave Angus hope Caleb would get through this all right. But now Caleb stared down at his hands on the table and muttered, "I don't want to talk about it."

Fine, Angus would circle around and get back to it. "So your dad has been able to find you repeatedly. How?"

Caleb drew an invisible pattern on the table with his finger. "He's smart. Between what he knows of my mom and his contacts in the shifter world..." He shrugged. "He figures it out. Though it took him eight months this last time."

"So he'll figure out Wolf Town too," Angus stated.

That brought Caleb's head up, and his startled gaze met Angus's. He knew what the boy was thinking—Angus would want to get rid of Caleb before that happened.

"I intend to be prepared for your father's arrival." Angus smiled. "You're not going anywhere, Caleb, if it's up to me. I hope you want to stay here for a while."

"I do," the boy replied fervently.

"Good. But you need to tell me about the last time your dad found you."

"I can't." That hoarse whisper and the strongest fear Angus had felt for days. He controlled his anger, not wanting to have Caleb react to it in any way.

"Okay, tell me why you can't speak of it."

"It was too *weird*," Caleb blurted.

Angus frowned, wishing he knew what that meant to Caleb.

"I'll tell you about the time before," Caleb offered, a little desperately.

"Why the time before?"

The boy paused, and resignation seemed to make his body sag. "I don't want to lie to you about the last time."

That night Rory dropped by after supper. Caleb had already met Angus's son once, but Rory was one of the most engaging, personable werewolves one could meet, so Angus figured Caleb would do well to meet him again.

Rory plopped down on the couch beside Caleb, close but not too close. "Hey, Caleb, my dad treating you okay?"

For a brief instant, Caleb glanced Angus's way, and his face seemed to shine.

"You can tell him the truth," Angus said as Caleb fumbled with actual words, looking for a way to respond to Rory.

Caleb frowned until he realized he was being teased and his expression lightened. With a slight eye roll, he mumbled a yes at Rory.

"Not doing too many dishes, I hope?"

Since Caleb had done zero dishes and the idea probably hadn't occurred to him, he looked a little puzzled. And concerned.

"Don't worry," Rory added with a sly smile. "Dad'll tell you when he wants you to do anything. He's good that way. I know you're just getting on your feet." Rory shifted so he leaned forward, elbows on his knees. "Did you know there's a school in town? Small, but definitely functioning."

Caleb slouched farther into the couch, although he appeared more tense, not less. With a brittle bravado that was all too telling, he stated, "School and I don't really get along all that well. I'm better off out of it."

Rory glanced at his father, then continued. "You're fifteen, right?"

"Yeah."

"Dad has to follow the rules of the government. They're more than happy for him to be the guardian of a young werewolf like yourself. But he can't have fifteen-year-olds hanging out with him when they're legally supposed to be in school."

Caleb's entire body seized up. "I don't want to get Angus in trouble."

Angus stepped in. "It's not just about the government, though Rory's right, that is a concern. We also want to think of your future."

The sullenness descended.

"When did you last go to school?" Rory asked.

Caleb put his hands together, began knocking his thumbs at each other. "I never did. Mom homeschooled me."

"How did that go?" At Rory's question, Caleb gave Angus a pleading expression, as if he wanted Angus to tell Rory to stop this line of inquiry.

But Angus stayed silent and Caleb reluctantly answered. "I wasn't the easiest kid to teach."

Blames himself, not his mother. With his brief, sideways glance at Angus, Rory saw it too. "Well, there's an assessment before you start. We can take you there tomorrow."

Caleb's face turned a deep embarrassed red, and a whiff of desperation came off him. "I'll flunk." He jumped up and started pacing, like he was locked in the house. "Look. I just want a place to rest a while, before my dad finds me. Don't tell the government, okay?"

Angus stood up and walked over. "Relax." He draped an arm over the boy's shoulders and Caleb leaned into him. "Do you think this is unusual? Lots of shifter kids get the short end of the stick when it comes to education. We've had kids who couldn't read at all. It's not about intelligence, it's about opportunity. We want to give you this opportunity."

In response, Caleb leaned into Angus more. "I can read," he mumbled, "but I'm slow."

"That's a start."

"I don't get math."

"When have you learned any math?"

Caleb sighed. "Mom didn't like teaching math."

"Well, there you go."

Rory stood too, putting down the empty cup of coffee he'd finished. "Our high school is small and flexible. I promise you, you won't feel out of place."

Caleb eyed him, clearly convinced Rory didn't know what he was talking about.

"Night, Caleb. I gotta get home."

Caleb nodded and detached himself from Angus, who gave Rory a hug. His son smelled of his boyfriend, Scott, which was all well and good. Scott might be the most skittish man Angus had ever met, but he was right for Rory.

Once he'd left, Jancis entered the room. "So, how'd it go?" she asked, which made it clear to Caleb that they'd planned the school talk.

Caleb simply looked at Angus, his big brown eyes filled with resignation.

"That good, huh?" She smiled. "Hey, if Aileen learned to read at seventeen, you can learn anything at the young age of fifteen, kid."

Aileen wasn't quite the example Angus wanted Caleb to emulate. She'd had one tough row to hoe and refused to accept some aspects of her humanity. But for better or worse, Caleb relaxed at Jancis's words. As if he believed he might not be out of place, as Rory had claimed.

There were moments after a nightmare when Mala felt like someone was watching her. It was crazy, given that in the dreams she was the one who climbed into someone else and talked to them—or attacked. Maybe this sensation was psychic payback. First she dreamed of having all this power, of taking control, and then she lost it in real life.

Never mind that the dreams were always wolves wolves wolves.

She should have been more shocked last year when the news hit the headlines about werewolves and that they really existed. It had been splashed over the front pages for weeks, making it hard to remain ignorant of them. Work had burbled over with conversation about wolves, until the boss had yelled at everyone to shut it.

But she hadn't been surprised by the shocking news, more appalled and unnerved that her dreams had known what no one in her life did. Nevertheless, she'd avoided reading too much about werewolves, when the reading material was everywhere, for fear she'd get obsessed about them in an even more unhealthy way. For fear that her own damaged brain would bring about more nightmares if they overran her waking existence.

All that said, she had vaguely heard of Wolf Town, of course she had, even if she'd tried to block it out, avoid the front pages and the big news stories. No wonder her subconscious had served up that name in her dream, giving it to Caleb to utter. Despite that logical conclusion, she could not convince herself it was all in her head. A week after she'd last "spoken" to Caleb, it felt like her only choice was to take a bus up north and...

And what?

That was the big question. Whatever was she going to accomplish? She could ask around for a Caleb. Would the inhabitants of Wolf Town appreciate that? Maybe not, but they wouldn't arrest her for the question either. If she got thrown out of town—could they do that?—so be it.

The bus rolled into the Toronto station, and she glanced around at the people milling near her, half-expecting someone to be bearing down upon her. Her paranoia was too strong, and she forced herself to shrug it off as she mounted the steps of the bus and handed over her ticket to North Bay. She'd overnight there, then catch the regional bus to Wolf Town.

If she'd had the money for a rental car, it might have been a smarter means of transportation. But she was a nervous driver and money was tight. The nightmares meant she lived alone, and an apartment in Toronto was not cheap, even a one-room basement apartment.

She walked down the narrow aisle of the bus and settled into a plush seat where she felt more comfortable. She had the double seat to herself and the backs were high enough to hide her from everyone's view.

No one is watching you, she reminded herself. *The only person watching is yourself.* She sometimes thought she was slowly driving herself crazy.

The closer Mala got to Wolf Town, the sillier she felt. She needed therapy, not a visit to the latest phenomenon in Ontario, if not all of North America. Gaping tourists were not encouraged, and after the first crush of them, there'd apparently been some beef up in town security. She'd been catching up on her reading about wolves during her week of unemployment. It had felt strangely thrilling to be reading about something she'd avoided this past year.

Her secret, unhappy dreamlike obsession—wolves. Lucky her. Why couldn't she obsess about...shoes or something? But no, wolves it was, in her dreams and in her nightmares.

She got off the bus, hiked her pack up on her back and walked out of the small station. They had more snow on the ground here than in Toronto, no surprise. She glanced up and down the main road to see it looked like every other small town in northern Ontario she'd just bussed through on the milk run. There were no wolves in sight. She wondered if she gave off an *I'm not a werewolf* vibe that would alienate everyone she talked to. But from what she'd read, the town had plenty of non-wolf inhabitants. Wolf Town attracted wolves *and* those with wolves in the family.

Two blocks down she identified a friendly looking restaurant and walked in. The waitress and all five customers turned to stare at her, and she had the impression one of them sniffed.

Courage. She pasted on a smile and marched up to the counter to drop her bag at her feet.

"Hi."

The woman nodded, and Mala had the same feeling she'd had on occasion when she realized she was the only dark-skinned person in a room full of whites and the whites all noticed. That wasn't the case here, but she felt out of place, an outsider. Well, for goodness' sake, she was an outsider. *Focus, Mala.*

"What would you like?" the waitress asked.

"Um." Oh yeah, she'd do well to look at the menu posted on

the chalkboard. She seized upon the first appealing item listed. "Tuna melt, please, and a coffee. Thanks very much."

"Coming up." The waitress didn't soften exactly, but Mala had the impression politeness had gone some way to ease the wariness in the restaurant. Which had Mala wondering if people here got tourists who came in saying rude things and asking stupid questions.

That said, she had *her* question to ask. But the waitress made it easy. As she delivered Mala's plate, she said, "Visiting someone in town?"

Shaking her head, Mala watched the waitress's mouth tighten. She was about to withdraw from Mala, and she didn't want to miss the opportunity. *Go for it. Take the plunge.* "But I am looking for a Caleb. A teenage boy."

She could feel her face burn. She knew what her blush looked like, a deep, unattractive red. It made her look awkward. In her embarrassment, it took Mala a moment to realize that although the waitress's eyes had narrowed, she hadn't answered, hadn't said something to the effect that she didn't know any such Caleb.

Good God, could the boy in her dreams somehow be real?

The waitress glanced sideways, meeting the gaze of a tall, dark woman who had risen from her table.

Grim-faced, the woman swept past Mala and out the glass door. Mala glanced from the door back to the waitress, unsure what was going on.

"Want some dessert with that?" the woman asked, her tone frosty. Her pale eyes held a flat expression.

"Um, no thanks." Mala was having trouble interpreting what had just happened. It wasn't that awful a question, surely? But the atmosphere had turned creepy, with the waitress looking at her like she was something to wipe off the bottom of her shoe and the customers who remained burning holes in her back. Or so she imagined. Mala's imagination liked to go into overdrive. The source of all her problems, her father used to tell her with some regularity.

She went with a perky, vacant tone. "I'll pay up now." She handed over her credit card.

"Why thank you," said the waitress with an excess of sarcasm, and took the card, leaving for the kitchen instead of going to the cash register.

Mala snuck a glance at the customers who all suddenly found something to talk about. She really wanted to leave, right away. There'd been stories, of course, stories she'd disregarded, where people claimed Wolf Town was a dangerous place to visit with out-of-control wolves ready to attack at any moment.

She hadn't been able to believe the government would sanction such a place. Maybe she'd been naïve. She leaned forward on the counter and called out, "Excuse me?"

Though she could see the waitress's back, the older woman didn't respond or turn around. In fact, she picked up her cell and began talking. Mala felt trapped and she didn't think it was an accident. Perhaps she should take her losses and leave without her credit card. Except money was a bit of an issue for her.

The door slammed open then, and she spun on her seat to face a large, broad-shouldered man who strode towards her with purpose. She wanted to pull her own fear together, shape it into a weapon and strike him down—except this wasn't a dream. So she rose to standing and braced herself, though for what, she couldn't imagine.

He pulled up short and leaned down to inhale deeply. He held that breath and while he did, his eyes, a vivid blue, changed from angry to...bemused. He blinked once before he exhaled.

"Can I help you?" she asked as coolly as possible. She didn't like gazing up at him as he stood above her, too close, and she was *not* used to strange men sniffing her. She didn't care if that was the norm in this town—along with stealing credit cards.

"I hope so." His mouth curved up on one side, an attractive warm expression at total odds with the determined, flat look he'd worn as he'd first entered the restaurant, and she found herself overwhelmed by his mere presence. "But first, let me welcome you to Wolf Town."

Chapter Four

She stood at such attention that Angus almost expected a salute. He'd come in here a tad angry, yes. Jancis announcing that someone was after Caleb hadn't put Angus in the most welcoming frame of mind. But this young woman was a) not a werewolf, b) frightened and c) smelled good.

Okay, she did smell good to him in an appealing she-attracts-me way. Not that it mattered since she was human. But he meant to focus on the fact his nose told him she was on the side of good. His most famed characteristic in the world of shifters was his nose, which managed to suss out when someone was essentially a decent person. Or not.

This dark-eyed young lady with hacked-off hair—was it the style these days?—did not deliberately do people harm.

So perhaps she'd been coerced or manipulated into this. Or perhaps she was being followed unawares. Maybe Caleb knew her. Angus didn't believe in coincidence.

He realized he'd been circling her and she was trembling, her heart rate not only increasing but accelerating. Obviously his words of welcome couldn't be taken quite at face value. And his actions were too wolf-like to be comfortable for a normal.

He backed off to sit on a stool two over from where she'd been seated. Then he cut to the chase. "I'm Angus MacIntyre. I'd like to know why you're visiting us here in Wolf Town."

Her eyes widened. Recognition of his name, he assumed, given that newspaper articles and such tended to mention him as the one in charge. Some even called him a mayor.

She glanced behind her where, yes, everyone was staring, all five of them. Could be she expected to be attacked. While he disliked some of the assumptions normals made about wolves, he also didn't intend to bait this woman. He wanted to know about her connection to Caleb.

He could see what it was like for her. She wondered if she'd made a terrible mistake, if she'd stumbled into some kind of trouble she didn't know how to get out of.

She also didn't know how to lie, because whatever she was trying to say didn't come out. Finally the stiff set of her shoulders relaxed in a kind of surrender, though she remained standing.

To the customers and Eden watching, he called out, "I'm trying to have a private conversation here." They turned away, not that they wouldn't hear everything anyway, but a semblance of privacy had its uses. To the strange woman, he said, "No one is going to cause you harm in this town. But you've shown an interest in one of my people and *that* interests me."

Her mouth dropped open and the surprise, almost shock, was real. "Caleb is here?"

"Caleb who?"

"Yes." She appeared to forget she'd been frightened moments earlier, her intense interest in Caleb surpassing everything else. And it wasn't malevolent interest, he was sure of it. Maybe she'd been sent by Caleb's mother? Though Shanna hadn't tried very hard to reach out to Caleb since they'd decided to separate to survive Caleb's father. Angus disapproved of her lack of effort, though he didn't intend to disparage Caleb's one non-psychotic parent in front of the boy.

"Yes," the strange woman repeated. "There are many Calebs in the world." A line formed between her eyes and she asked the question like so much was riding on it. "He's not a young boy, is he? A teenager, I mean. He's not..." her voice dropped to a whisper, as if she could barely believe she was saying the words aloud, "...a skinny black wolf?"

He stared at her. Because of course Caleb was a skinny black wolf, and wouldn't she be sure of that if she was searching for him? Why would she be looking for someone she didn't know? He let the silence build, waiting to see if she'd say more. But when he didn't answer, she seemed to come to a conclusion and covered her mouth with her fist. Her next words made even less sense.

"Oh my God, he's *real?*" she said, aghast.

"And then she fell down," Angus concluded.

"Fell down?" Jancis maintained her skeptical expression.

"She just kind of stumbled. I extended a hand to help her, and she evaded me, missed the stool she was reaching for and...fell down." Angus felt a bit bad about that. He should have realized she wasn't ready for him to steady her physically, but he'd been so struck by her reaction that he wasn't thinking with all cylinders firing. At that point he considered and rejected the idea of offering her a hand up, and she'd pulled herself to standing with the help of a stool.

"I've got a wild idea," Rory put in. "Why don't we ask Caleb if he knows this woman. You say her name is Mala?"

Jancis rolled her eyes at her brother who grinned back.

"We plan to," Angus said dryly. "I'd rather talk to Caleb

first, when he's done with school for the day. Meanwhile, Mala is getting settled in one of Eden's rooms. She was a little reluctant—"

"Eden or Mala?" interrupted Rory.

"Both."

Jancis shook her head. "I don't know why Eden even runs a B and B if she doesn't want people to stay in it."

"She wants people to stay, but only those she knows." Angus waved a hand. "We're getting off track here."

"What's this strange woman's last name?" asked Jancis.

"She didn't say."

"Isn't that suspicious?"

"We're already suspicious." Angus paused. He knew his kids weren't crazy when he did this, came up with a judgment based on his nose. But it had yet to steer him wrong. "Thing is, she smells good."

For a moment both of them were the twins they'd always been, and their expressions became identical and close to resigned, a silent *Okay, Dad, we can't argue with that.*

They believed him, unlike some people, but Rory didn't see why his nose wasn't as infallible as Angus's—though he had good gut reactions with people and Angus thought that was partly why—and Jancis preferred to remain suspicious of all outsiders. So her countenance became even more disgruntled than it had been.

Angus shot her a look. "Better than if she smelled of bad intent, Jancis, don't you think? For Caleb's sake."

"Of course." Jancis propped her hands on her hips. "But this means you won't want to get rid of her, and I'd rather she wasn't around."

"We're supposed to interact with outsiders," Angus said

mildly. "We're a town, not an island. If we never interact, people will become crazy suspicious and the government will feel they have to do something."

"She smells good," Rory repeated, bringing them back to Mala. He cocked his head. "Do you think she's in trouble then?"

Angus shrugged. "She's scared."

"Of Caleb?" asked Jancis.

"Maybe, or something about Caleb. Maybe Caleb's father threatened her too." Angus spread out his hands to indicate he didn't know, and he realized he'd just brought his daughter on board for trying to get to know Mala better. Jancis didn't like *anyone* to be threatened. She was as protective as any wolf he knew.

Rory, in the end, was the more insightful one, at least on a personal level. There was a slight drawl as he asked, "So, Dad, what do *you* think of her?"

Angus was not willing to explain to his kids that he was attracted to the falling-down stranger with wide eyes and an appealing scent. Besides, he didn't do attraction these days, especially instant attraction. Didn't have time for it. Furthermore, he preferred wolves, always had.

Nevertheless, he had to answer Rory's question.

"I think Mala is here on some sort of quest and wants questions answered. She doesn't lie easily. I even suspect, given her reaction, that the actual meeting with Caleb will be something of a jolt. The idea of him makes her nervous."

"Sounds strange," Jancis muttered, and Angus shrugged.

"Well, we should arrange it," said Rory. "Since she smells good and is apparently harmless. If she was going to tell someone Caleb was here, she already would have, I'd think. Besides we're not a secret or odd place for a werewolf to land."

Angus inclined his head in agreement. "We'll arrange it, not immediately though. I want to give Caleb good warning in case he knows her or knows of her. Jancis, we'll need you about so this young woman doesn't end up surrounded by a bunch of strange wolf men sniffing her. That's not the atmosphere I want today." Or any day. The idea got Angus's back up.

This time it was Jancis who drawled. "You're calling her a young woman?"

Angus raised his eyebrow. "Is there something wrong with that description? Perhaps you would prefer I describe her as a young lady?"

Jancis shook her head at him. "She's older than us, Dad."

Angus wasn't interested in trying to understand his daughter's point. That Rory grinned again made Angus sigh. "You two. Remember when you were nine?"

Rory had decided Angus and his teacher should get married. Never mind that the teacher, though liking Angus well enough, had no interest in men.

"That was Rory, not me," Jancis pointed out. "You use 'young woman' to make it sound like there's some huge age difference between you two instead of a decade."

"Do I? Any other important and incisive psychological observations you'd like to make while you're at it?"

"Nope." Jancis smiled a lot less often than her brother, but Angus liked to see it. "Who's going to break it to Caleb that someone's looking for him?"

"Me," said Angus. "I'll be heading over to the school. You go make friends with Mala—"

"Right." Jancis's smile faded.

"—and I'll call you when you should bring Mala to the house."

"Anything you want of me?" asked Rory.

"You observe when we all get back," Angus said. "Sometimes you see things we don't."

"I'll make coffee and wait then," called Rory, as Angus and Jancis headed out the door.

Jancis muttered, "Why does he get the easy jobs, that's what I'd like to know. He makes coffee and I have to babysit. I don't *like* talking to strange women."

"You'll do great," Angus declared, and watched his daughter set her jaw.

"I sure as hell wasn't looking for a pep talk, Dad. That was a complaint about division of labor in our family."

"You complain, I give pep talks, that's how it goes." He lowered his voice. "I need you for this, Jancis."

She huffed out a breath of exasperation, but strode off in the direction of Eden's B and B.

"Let me know if there's anything else I can do for you." The waitress who'd stolen her credit card had been coaxed into giving it back to Mala by Angus MacIntyre. Unfortunately, that was not the end of their dealings, because the waitress had then been put in charge of lodging Mala in her B and B.

To think her name, and that of the B and B, was Eden. The irony was rich, but Mala wasn't comfortable enough to appreciate it.

There apparently wasn't much in the way of hotels around here. Mala hadn't reserved a room before arrival because she'd imagined catching the afternoon bus back to North Bay after learning no one had ever heard of any Caleb.

That hadn't happened.

The dream kept coming back to her. It wasn't that she had

a clear idea of what he looked like as a boy. When he'd been human, she'd seen through his eyes but not into his eyes.

Whereas she'd seen him through his father's gaze, right after she'd attacked the large wolf. Caleb's wolf eyes were brown, his fur black.

In her dream.

Could it have been real?

She rubbed her arms, the fear of being crazy taking strong hold of her. It was not the time for a panic attack. She was among strangers who regarded her with suspicion, who clearly feared she might be a threat to their Caleb.

What a joke. She'd never been more useless in her life. Out of a job, in a small, strange town on a wild-goose chase, estranged from her family... She wasn't in a position to threaten anyone, was she?

Someone rapped at the door and Mala shot to standing.

"Yes?" she said with more authority than she felt.

Eden marched in with a glare, and clean sheets landed on the bed where Mala had been sitting.

"Anything else?" Eden demanded.

"Uh, no, that's great." Mala forced out a smile. "Thank you." She hoped to sound dismissive without being rude. After all, Eden wasn't happy in her company, and Mala needed time alone during this mini-meltdown.

"You wait here."

Mala blinked. "For...?"

"Jancis is coming over."

Then Eden slammed the door shut and Mala stared at it. Who the hell was Jancis?

It didn't take long for Mala's question to be answered.

About ten minutes later there came a light knock on her door. Rather gingerly, Mala opened it, expecting Eden might have returned to dump towels on her bed or something.

There were towels, but another woman held them. She was tall, slim and serious-faced. Beautiful in a remote way. Holding out her free hand, she said, "Hello, I'm Jancis MacIntyre, Angus's daughter."

Wow, he was older than he looked if his daughter was in her mid-twenties or so. Maybe werewolves didn't really age, although that was supposed to be a myth.

Mala took her hand. "Mala Singh."

With that, Jancis handed over the towels and glanced at Mala's bed. "Hmm. Eden doesn't like you or she would have stayed to make your bed."

At a loss, Mala nodded. How was she supposed to respond to such an observation? Suddenly she recognized this Jancis as the woman who'd left the café right after Mala had asked after Caleb. Jancis had summoned Angus, her father, who'd marched up to Mala in a rather intimidating fashion. Just great. Mala's face burned at the memory of falling on her ass right at Angus's feet.

At least he'd had the decency not to laugh at her.

Jancis tilted her head. "Want to go for a walk? I'll show you the sights."

No, Mala did not want to go for a walk with this woman. She didn't even want to be here. But she had to follow this through, and Jancis was her link to Caleb so she couldn't blow her off. "I thought I was going to meet Caleb."

"You will." Jancis's tone suggested there was no doubt about this. "He needs a bit of preparation."

"Oh?" Mala couldn't imagine what preparation was involved

in meeting her. Sure, she was crazy but no one here knew that. Yet.

"It's hard to explain." Jancis jerked her thumb towards the door. "Come on, we have an hour to kill before he's out of school anyway. You don't want to just sit in this room."

Yes. I do. "There's no need for you to waste your time spending it with me."

Jancis's unsmiling gaze turned assessing. "Oh, I think you'll be more comfortable with me around so you don't have strange men sniffing after you."

Mala couldn't tell by the wry quirk of Jancis's lips if she was being truthful or trying to unnerve her—mocking some of Mala's fears. They wouldn't seek her out in her room, would they?

"And I promise I'll take you to Caleb. If you stick with me."

Well, maybe Jancis's company was the best route to go. Mala didn't want to miss the opportunity to meet this possible boy from her dream, so she'd be amenable.

"It's chilly. I'd bring your winter coat."

Jancis was younger than her and Mala was fully aware of how cold it was outside. But she tamped down her irritation, picked up her coat and followed the Wolf Town resident outside.

Angus went into the school, newly renovated, since the government had agreed with him that education was critical for young wolves. The masses weren't bloodthirsty enough to try to eradicate all werewolves, not with a number of them being children, so the next best thing was to bring them into the mainstream a little more. In the past, homeschooling had been the recourse of many parents raising their children, and while that worked for some, it had been a disaster for others.

Caleb wasn't too badly off. His education was uneven at best, and he might be behind in a lot of things, but Angus had met illiterate teenagers who were a lot more disadvantaged.

It helped that Caleb was bright.

He waited until the bell rang. Caleb was still unsure enough to be rattled by Angus marching into the classroom. Only after the boy left his locker did Angus approach him in the hall.

Caleb came to a full stop, clearly wondering if something was wrong.

Angus smiled and kept his tone casual. "Come with me. I have something a bit strange to tell you."

Caleb obeyed, following him out and looking up at him. Angus had the impression that the boy had grown since he'd arrived, but it was too soon for that, even for a werewolf. However, the pinched, starved appearance had disappeared. Caleb remained a skinny teenager but he was filling out thanks to regular meals.

"Strange?" asked Caleb. "Strange how?"

"I've a question for you first. Have you ever met someone named Mala?"

"Mala?" That evidently wasn't anywhere near what Caleb had expected Angus to say, and he looked nonplussed. "No. I've never heard of that name."

"She's about your height, late twenties say. I'd guess a South Asian background, dark eyes and shoulder-length hair." Angus watched Caleb's puzzled expression. "Doesn't ring any bells?"

"No."

Angus stopped and placed a reassuring hand on that bony shoulder. "Did your father ever send women out to find you?"

Caleb's expression shuttered, and it hurt to see him close up at the mention of his father. In a low voice, he said, "No."

"That's what I thought." Angus gave that shoulder a reassuring shake, and they started walking again. "She seems harmless. In fact, she seems a bit...lost. So I'd be surprised if there's a direct link to your father. But I felt I should check with you, ask your opinion."

Caleb nodded, gratitude shining in his eyes. It meant a lot to him when Angus took his opinions seriously. "Only guys, only wolves searched me out. My dad doesn't have much to do with anyone else."

"All right. Anyway, she wants to meet you. When I asked for her reason, she said, 'I'd rather not say.' Jancis might have gotten more information out of her." Angus glanced down. "How would you feel about meeting this Mala?"

"I don't care."

Angus smiled. Sullen, sounding like a teenager, and he probably *didn't* care. Caleb's distress had ebbed since Angus had described Mala. She was no one to him at this point. "Okay, I'll give Jancis a call when we get home."

They arrived shortly, and Rory, who'd made coffee and was ready for company, started an argument with Caleb about hockey. Not about which team was better, since Caleb hadn't watched much hockey in his life, but whether or not it was a stupid sport. Caleb apparently only liked football. Angus retreated from the voices and picked up the kitchen phone. Jancis answered her cell on the second ring.

"So?" he asked. "Get anything more out of her?"

"No. Give me a moment."

He waited.

"Okay, she can't hear me. She won't say why she wants to

see Caleb but seems embarrassed about it."

"Interesting." He'd picked up Mala's embarrassment earlier but had thought it generalized.

"And she's said more than once that our Caleb is probably not someone she knows."

"It doesn't add up, Jancis."

"Yeah. Well. I'm not sure *she* adds up, if you get my drift."

"Okay. Bring her over. See what happens."

"I bet it'll be anticlimactic."

Angus grunted and hung up. He should be agreeing with Jancis, agreeing this was nothing. But his gut instinct said he was about to learn something big.

And he never ignored his instinct.

Chapter Five

It would be five minutes max before Jancis and Mala arrived, and that was only if Mala's walking speed was glacial. So Angus stood in the doorway between the kitchen and living room and watched Caleb raise his voice and swing his arm as he explained why football, with its strategy, was much better than a game where guys skated around on ice together.

Angus smiled, and his concern for Caleb eased. Yes, there was something to this Mala woman, but it might not have much to do with Caleb. He hoped not. He'd prefer Caleb's life stay as simple as possible for the time being.

The boy hadn't wanted to start at the school, and Angus's heart had broken for him a little as he trudged over that first morning. Fortunately, Harrison, the principal, had proved once again that he was just what the school needed, easing Caleb into the resource room for the preliminary tests and then into the classes themselves the next day.

Caleb didn't go as far as saying he liked school, but after a few days he no longer looked as if he were off to face the executioner each morning.

The doorbell rang. A warning on Jancis's part, since she lived here. The two women walked in—Jancis's expression bland though Angus could sense an uneasiness about her, and Mala's body tense, as if bracing herself for the worst of news.

That put him on edge. Angus strolled over to the front door. "Get a tour of the town?" he asked Mala.

She crossed her arms as she stood even straighter. "Yes, thank you."

Jancis took Mala's coat to hang up. "She's a bit cold, I think. I'll put on some tea." She glanced towards the living room. "Soon."

Hearing the voices, Mala edged forward, and Angus watched until she stared at him in question. It was all a bit odd, including the intense expression on her face, but they might as well get it over with.

"Come in." He took her elbow. Her thin arm fit in his palm nicely, and he observed that she didn't resist his hand on her, lightly guiding.

Seated on the couch, Caleb looked up and did a once-over of Mala. There was no recognition on his face. *Good.*

But at seeing Caleb, Mala stiffened under Angus's hand and stood straighter, if that was possible. The pulse in her neck became visible, and she raised her fist to her mouth, that same gesture she'd used at Eden's when she'd asked if Caleb was real.

She crumpled without warning, without a murmur. Only the increased weight on his palm enabled Angus to move in time and catch her before she hit the ground.

"Hey," said Rory in concern. He jumped off the couch while Caleb's mouth dropped open.

Angus scooped her up, one arm under her legs, the other at her back, cradling her so her head didn't loll. Such a light weight. He wasn't used to this type of body—soft, not terribly muscular, non-wolf. He tried not to notice her scent, mild lavender and under that, Mala herself. She smelled not only good but appealing. Appealing—it had been a long while.

Not now. Of all the times for attraction to rear its head, in a room full of his kids and an unconscious woman. Jesus. He sure knew how to pick his moments.

"Off the couch," he demanded of Caleb, who leapt up. "Thank you," Angus added more softly, not pleased that he was snapping at the boy. "I just want to be able to lay her down."

Rory pulled away the coffee table and Angus knelt, Mala now stirring. He didn't want to put her down. She seemed to fit in his arms, actually curling into him a little. But they had company, and he had her reaction to Caleb to assess, so he laid her out on the couch with care.

She hadn't meant to fall asleep, and panic hit her hard. It was too soon—

No, wrong place, wrong situation. She wasn't at home in her bed, she wasn't trying to avoid a recent night terror by staying awake. But she *was* confused. Her eyelashes fluttered opened to meet the strong blue gaze of...Angus, alpha of Wolf Town.

What the hell was she doing lying down beside him?

"Okay?" He touched her forehead lightly, moving bangs away.

She shouldn't like his hand on her. She didn't know him and she despised people who went touchy-feely on her.

Instead she wanted him to touch her again. How odd.

"Mala?" he asked.

She looked past him to see three more people staring down at her. One was young and, oh God, it all came back—one was *him.*

She didn't know how she recognized Caleb exactly, but recognition it was, like in those dreams where you know someone you've never met in real life. Only this was all backwards and mixed up.

Scrubbing her eyes was a way of temporarily blocking out the gazes of four people who all seemed concerned to some degree. Caleb maybe least of all.

She forced herself to sit up, and Angus edged back, going from his crouch beside her to sitting on the coffee table.

"Mala," Angus asked, "would you prefer a glass of orange juice or apple juice?"

She wanted neither but, locked in his gaze, felt obligated to choose one out of politeness. "Apple."

"Caleb, can you get that please?"

The boy left the room, and for a moment, Mala was able to breathe again. *Oh my God. Am I making this up? Am I finally going crazy?*

She didn't want to lose her mind.

"Relax." Angus's voice was so reassuring, so mellow and deep. She stared, getting lost in that careful regard of his. "You're safe here." His mouth quirked up. "I promise."

Caleb returned and, with it, that feeling of familiarity. She knew him from her dream, the recognition stirred deep within her. He stood there, not sure who to give the glass to until Angus reached out and took it. He passed it on to Mala and said, "Drink. It will be good for your blood sugar."

It was too sweet, apple juice usually was, but the taste wasn't so bad.

When she was done, Angus retrieved the empty glass from her, and she glanced around the room again. Jancis seemed impatient, Caleb restless. There was another man present who looked a lot like Jancis, but he'd settled into a chair to read a magazine as if nothing was going on.

"Okay?" Angus asked a second time.

"Yes." She cleared her throat and went to push up to standing, but stopped when Angus laid a staying hand on her arm. His palm was warm through the cotton of her long-sleeved shirt, and suddenly she couldn't move, couldn't do anything but soak up his heat. Something strange and foreign flushed through her and she recognized it as attraction.

Oh God, she thought rather forlornly. Her ability to be attracted to anyone had rusted out years ago. Yet, here she was, mesmerized by the blunt, strong fingers touching her arm.

"Whoa," he said, bringing her focus back to the present situation. He took that hand away, and she realized he was referring to her standing, not to her reaction to his touch. "Do me the favor of sitting here for a while. We don't want you falling down a third time while I'm right beside you. You'll give me a complex."

She couldn't respond to his charming half-smile though a part of her wanted to. Wow, what a bad time to be completely dazzled by a man. She couldn't believe it. This never happened to her. *Never.* She'd given up on herself as too numb to respond to anyone, even mildly, let alone like this.

It was baffling, especially with Caleb in the room.

"Can I ask you a question?" Angus said.

No. "Okay," she answered.

"Do you know Caleb?"

At the question and Mala's regard, Caleb looked self-conscious, though he clearly didn't recognize her. And God knows what her recognition meant. While a part of her was so embarrassed, she just wanted to get out of here, another part was desperate to ask.

But ask what? And how? *Hey, Caleb, did your father*

brutalize you three weeks ago?

She was not going to ask such an awful question of him. No way.

Then she remembered her marker—the room, in her dream, when Caleb had been human, and that beautiful painting of three wolves hanging on the wall.

Angus was watching her, and when she turned back his way, she expected his patience to have run out for this spacey woman on his couch. But nothing of the sort showed on his face.

In fact, his expression encouraged her to blurt out, "Do you have a winter scene, wolves running together, three of them, up through the pine trees to the hill, the moon illuminating their way?"

Something wary flickered in his eyes, caution, and she recognized that she had started down the road towards showing too much of herself.

But what the hell. Complete strangers weren't going to force her into therapy, or worse. They might say good riddance, but they wouldn't get involved in her life.

"In a bedroom," she added.

"That's in my room," Caleb confirmed, and he was the one who seemed least surprised that she would know about the painting.

She was shaking again and she clamped her teeth together. The knowledge that it was real, that her dreaming was connected to the real world, threatened to overwhelm her. Caleb had offered her proof, even if he didn't know it.

"What's going on." It was a question, but delivered as a flat command, and the warmth had left Angus's face, his expression suggesting she might considered a threat to them.

Get yourself together. Her first reaction was to clam up. Whenever she'd tried to explain what was going on inside her head before, it had been disastrous. But these were wolves, for God's sakes, and she might have even helped Caleb.

She pushed up to standing, and immediately Angus loomed beside her. He no longer seemed friendly, but that didn't matter. Nothing mattered but understanding something about what her dreams meant.

"Where?" she asked Caleb, who looked to Angus for guidance.

"What are you trying to prove?" demanded Jancis.

Mala startled, having forgotten Jancis was in the room, given she was so focused on the wolf painting, and Caleb and Angus. But she answered the other woman. "I want to know why I saw that picture in my dream."

She stood as if waiting for a blow, the dark eyes even darker with something like fear but also anticipation. Angus loved that painting. Harrison had gifted it years ago, and Rory had asked for it to be hung in his bedroom back when Rory lived at home. It contained Angus, Rory and Trey as they headed out for a moonlight run.

The old urge to hide it was swift and strong, but werewolves were out and about now, and the painting was not going to give anyone away. Angus looked at Caleb. "Do you mind if she steps inside your room?"

From Caleb's face the answer was yes, but he just shrugged.

Angus tilted his head towards the hall. "Follow me."

"Me too?" Caleb asked.

"You too."

"Dream," Jancis said scathingly, watching as he led Mala to the room, and Mala's shoulders seemed to bow under some kind of weight.

Because Angus didn't dismiss anything, he tried to remember if there were any rumors of actual people having powers through dreams. He'd have to ask Trey what his take was. There were the occasional stories of dream wraiths, but Angus had put them in the same category as bogeymen and vampires. As werewolves, one got hit with a lot of bullshit.

For now, Angus tried to keep an open mind and gestured to the bedroom door that stood ajar. Mala took a deep breath then pushed the door open slowly, as if something inside the room might attack her. She walked in, gazing at...the bed of all things.

Caleb had made the bed, sort of, but it was nothing to stare at.

Angus had expected her to focus on the painting, but her back was to it.

"Caleb?" Her voice was thin, thready. Angus walked in so Caleb could follow him.

"Yeah," mumbled Caleb.

She pointed downward, and as she spoke, her voice was quiet, almost stuttering over her words. "You were sitting on this bed. You'd just woken up, and you were...unsure at first, but then you insisted that you were with friends, that I put away the weapon and go. So I did."

Angus disliked words like crazy and half-baked, which had been thrown too often at his people, so he was careful in his use of them on others. But he felt disappointment. This woman appeared to have problems.

"You also told me you were staying in Wolf Town. It's why I took a bus up here." The way she turned away from the bed and stared at the painting with a very slight smile curving her mouth, it made Angus sad. "I saw this painting before I left you." Her gaze cut to Caleb's. "Do you remember me? Is that possible?"

It was then that Angus smelled Caleb's confusion and fear. He'd been focused on Mala and hadn't noticed it building. Angus turned to the boy, put a hand on his shoulder to steady him, but Caleb's entire world had zeroed in on Mala.

"You?" he whispered, brown eyes wide. Not recognition, exactly, but her words meant something to him.

She nodded. "Yes. I believe so."

"Before too, that other time..." His voice went low and he had trouble finding the words. "With my dad..."

Again she nodded, solemn-faced and looking like she understood what Caleb was describing.

He cleared his throat. "After you helped me get away from him, did you...did you kill my dad?"

She shook her head, that lost expression creeping back on her face. "I stayed as long as possible, kept him down as long as possible. But whether I killed him..." She lifted a hand, palm up, gesturing her uncertainty. "I have no idea."

They gazed at each other, clearly making sense of the conversation between themselves, even if Angus didn't. Then Mala shrugged. "You see, Caleb, I didn't understand, until now, that it was more than a dream."

Chapter Six

"All right." Angus sat at the kitchen table, obviously trying to hang on to his temper. "Let's go through this again."

"This is *such* crap," said Jancis.

While Angus might be used to holding his temper, Mala wasn't. She rarely had to, because in day-to-day life she didn't tend to build up enough steam. But for the first time in her life she had proof that what she did in her dreams was somehow real, and this woman called it crap.

"Utter and complete crap."

Mala slammed a palm on the table and shoved up to standing. Unfortunately, she was four inches shorter than Jancis and her delivery was marred by a slight stutter as she started speaking. "Y-you don't know what you're talking about."

"Neither do you. You're making this up because—" Jancis threw out her hands, as if no explanation could be found for Mala's behavior.

"Don't forget to add the..." Mala spun a finger in a circle near her temple. "Think I haven't seen that one before?"

Jancis blinked once. "I don't care. All I know is you're messing with Caleb."

Caleb was tracing the wood table with his index finger. He'd drawn in on himself, was hunched and unhappy. Mala couldn't tell if it was because she didn't know if she'd killed his father or because rehashing that awful night was the last thing he wanted to do.

"She helped me escape," Caleb muttered.

Jancis sliced her gaze at Caleb and back to Mala, accusing. As if Mala was trying to ingratiate herself here by claims of heroism. Sure! That's how you impressed people. Tell them your dreams had the ability to enter the real life of their ward. People were always happy to hear that.

Suddenly, it was all too much, and Mala leaned on the table, feeling out of breath. She didn't want to leave Caleb. His existence and her finding him had opened a door into herself she hadn't known existed. She felt bonded to him, though maybe that emotion was all on her side. However, the rest of them, with their assessing gazes—she found the situation oppressive.

"I sliced into his heart," Mala said to her hands. It was hard to look, even at Caleb.

"You were white light. Sharp," Caleb mumbled, barely audible, but her relief was huge. He knew, he understood what had happened as well as she did. Which perhaps wasn't saying much.

She wasn't going to describe how she had fashioned herself into a weapon by feeding on Caleb's emotions. She didn't think anyone was ready to hear that yet and it sounded predatory. Vampirish even. And she was pretty darned sure she wasn't a vampire.

"Then you told me to run." Caleb's brown eyes stared into hers and she nodded.

So Caleb had heard her as she'd sat within his father and done the equivalent of screaming at him to run, hoping he'd flee, not knowing how long his father would be down for the count. "Yes."

"Then what happened?" It was Angus speaking, and it shook Mala out of her reverie.

Mala pulled in a breath, wondering how it would sound. But she had to say it. Caleb was there and he deserved to know the truth as she understood it. "I stopped his father's heart for as long as I could."

"Jesus." Jancis gestured at Mala. "It's like those woo-woo witches who wanted to cast shapeshifting spells on me last year by dancing under the full moon."

Angus pinched the bridge of his nose. "Jancis. You are not helping."

"I was there. *I was there.*" Caleb glared at Angus, eyes shiny.

Angus placed his large hand on top of Caleb's. "I know."

Mala pushed away from the table. "I'm going back to my room."

"No need," said Angus casually, and a shiver ran through Mala, a fear that he'd block her leaving. And who would ever know but the other residents of Wolf Town, none of whom she could trust. He watched her, eyebrows lifting, before he added, "You're welcome to stay at my house."

"All the same, I think I'll go." She breathed easier when he nodded in response.

"I'll walk you over to the B and B."

"No need," she echoed back to him.

"I'd like to ask you something in private."

Rather ungraciously, she shrugged. "Caleb." She waited until the boy looked at her. "I hope I can see you again, when I'm not so tired."

He too looked exhausted, as if this revelation was an

69

ordeal. "Okay."

Angus followed her out of the kitchen and down the hall, and she couldn't see how to prevent him from accompanying her. As she went to get her jacket, Angus spoke quietly to Jancis's brother, and Mala began to imagine a plot of some sort.

She felt vulnerable, that was the thing. If she could do this, what did it mean? What would people do to her? It sank in that she had revealed too much of herself too precipitously. Her father's old words, *You just don't think*, echoed through her.

She didn't want these people to know what she'd done, but she'd needed to determine if what she dreamed was real or not. Now she knew. And they knew.

Though given how erratic her dreams were, she couldn't be of much actual use or threat to anyone. Nothing about her dreams and nightmares was planned.

As she put on her boots, some similar ideas must have run through Angus's mind because he told Caleb, Jancis and Rory, "What's occurred and been discussed here today doesn't go outside this house. Not now."

Jancis scoffed.

His voice went hard, not a tone he had used on Mala. "I couldn't be more serious."

"My lips are sealed," Jancis drawled, not cowed, but not defiant either.

Though it felt awkward, Mala called out, "Bye, Caleb." She wanted to say she was glad to have met him in person, but that said so little of what she felt.

Caleb came to stand in the hall and gave an awkward nod while Angus stepped up to her. Mala found she was bracing herself, but Angus only pulled on boots, grabbed his jacket and gestured to her to lead the way outside.

Shoulders straight, Mala marched ahead of him, distress seeming to waft off her. He didn't know what to make of her, but no way in hell was he letting her leave Wolf Town until he better understood what was going on.

That meant being smart, because if she got the idea he'd block her departure... Well, that would be bad.

He came abreast of her and she glanced up sharply, but it was easy to see the uncertainty underneath. Jancis disliked outsiders, more protective of her werewolf brethren than the werewolves themselves. Despite his daughter's suspicions, Angus didn't think Mala was messing with Caleb—or anyone else.

She believed in her dream. And, tellingly, so did Caleb.

"How long?" Angus asked.

She rubbed her nose. "I arrived this morning."

"How long have you had these dreams?"

She laughed, no humor in it. "All my life."

"So...there have been others besides Caleb who you've met in your dreams?"

Instead of answering she sped up her gait, fast for someone who wasn't tall, though her steps were easy enough for him to keep pace with. "Don't worry," she said briskly. "No one else takes my dreams seriously. I don't expect you to."

He placed a hand on her shoulder and she stopped. But she didn't flinch or move away, which he found interesting. In a wolf, that would indicate a certain level of trust. Slowly he turned her to face him. "Believe me. I am taking this very seriously."

Those dark expressive eyes searched his face. "You daughter isn't impressed by me."

"No," he allowed. "She's protective of Caleb. And I think it's obvious that one scenario could be you're somehow playing games with him."

Her mouth twisted in dismay. "I would never do that."

"Good." He offered her a slight smile. "I didn't think you would."

"I am not cruel. Not intentionally. I wouldn't..."

There was only truth coming from her, and distress at the accusation. "I believe you."

She blinked. "Why?"

He grinned. "I can smell your sincerity."

At first she laughed, but under his steady gaze she started to look unsure. "You're joking, right?"

"Not at all." He released her and guided her forward. She wasn't dressed that warmly, and a sharp wind blew through town today.

After a pause, she moved again, rubbing a hand across her eyes as she did so. "I'm overwhelmed. I need some time alone to think."

"Let's get you some food from Eden to take up to your room."

"No!" She collected herself. "I mean, I'm not hungry."

"You can eat the food later." It was clear to Angus that Mala didn't want to deal with the B and B's proprietor. "Eden takes some getting used to, that's all. I'll come with you. We don't want you to fade away to nothing while you're with us." He ushered her into the restaurant that sat below Mala's room, and convinced Eden to get her guest a meal, his treat.

Mala endured a few suspicious glances but no outright scowls, and in fact, her wilting visibly seemed to take the edge off Eden's dislike. By the time Mala was settled in her room,

Angus knew he had to leave, her body posture was screaming at him to do so, though he wanted to ask her more questions.

But it was critical he not frighten her away. He didn't want her running, and he most certainly didn't want to chase her, not that way. If he managed this right, it would be more of a courtship than a predator-prey scenario.

"Okay?" he asked, and saw relief in her gaze when she realized he was about to leave her alone.

"Yes. Thank you for your help," she said, all politeness. She was a polite young woman. Too bad she wasn't a wolf. Of course, if she were, she probably wouldn't have these dreams. At least, Angus had never heard of a wolf displaying this power.

Then again, he'd never heard of *anyone* with this power. "Can we talk more this evening or tomorrow morning?"

"Tomorrow," she said quickly. "I really am quite worn out. I'm not used to traveling." She pulled a face, like she wished she hadn't confided that small piece of information.

He kept his tone mild. "Breakfast, then. Would you prefer Eden's restaurant or my kitchen?"

She hesitated, clearly feeling caught between a rock and a hard place.

"It's more private at my house. And I'll introduce you to Aileen. She's friendlier than the women you've met so far."

"Aileen," she said faintly, as if not up to meeting someone else.

"She was my ward before she grew up."

"Like Caleb."

"Like Caleb," he agreed. He moved away. "I'll pick you up at nine thirty tomorrow morning." Not giving her a chance to say no, he shut the door.

As he exited the building he saw Aileen, in wolf form,

across the street. Rory had got on it right away. When someone needed to be kept watch on, Angus and Rory turned to Aileen, who preferred being wolf to all else, more than any wolf he'd ever met, save ferals. Aileen had the first eight-hour shift with Mala. The two young women hadn't been introduced, but a stranger in town, staying at Eden's, was not going to be difficult for Aileen to identify.

Angus walked over, and Aileen leaned against his leg, letting him rub the top of her head. "Rory will give you a break at midnight."

She whined a protest, like Angus was suggesting she wasn't up for the entire job.

"Because I need you to sleep and get over to my place by nine fifteen tomorrow morning. Human form."

To show her displeasure, she growled. She didn't like being human, still, after all these years, but Angus worked to find reasons to force her human side to stay active. "This young lady, Mala, who Rory's told you about, will have breakfast at my place. She'll be more comfortable if another woman is present, since I'm a strange man to her. Okay?"

The woof held a question in it, even as she acceded to his request.

"Jancis doesn't like her. Eden doesn't like her. I like her, though, and if it's possible for you to at least not not like her, that would be a step forward."

Aileen licked his hand and trotted back to her post.

"See you tomorrow morning. I promise you lots of food."

Chapter Seven

That night Mala was scared to fall asleep. Though her thoughts were racing so hard that maybe she wouldn't have been able to sleep anyway.

What did it all mean? A part of her had always felt the dreams were too real and full of meaning to be only a product of her strange mind. Now she had proof she was right. She should have felt vindicated. But the idea of marching up to her parents, especially her father, and saying, *See, Papa, those weren't just night terrors...* Well, that scenario was never going to play out in any way that was satisfying to her.

Either she wouldn't be believed, the most likely outcome, or if she was, they'd be horrified that she was part of the paranormal crowd.

In her mind, she went over the Denizens of the Paranormal World—that had been the title of one article published right after werewolves had been presented to the world. As far as Mala knew, she fit in with nothing she'd read about. There were shifters, primarily wolves though the rare big cat was rumored to exist. And there were Minders, people who could bend other people's minds to their wills. Both groups were disliked, but Minders had the worse rap. They preyed on people whereas shifters mostly wanted to be left alone.

If that article was correct.

She should have read more before she'd hared off from Toronto and made her way north. Part of her wished to scurry home, and maybe she would, but she'd have breakfast with Angus first. She wanted to see Caleb again.

She worried about the boy, well, young man, and what he'd been through. She'd known his fear up close and personal, and that wasn't what any teenager should have gone through.

Perhaps something to talk to Angus, his guardian, about. The idea that Caleb had Angus to watch over him warmed Mala.

But that brought Mala back to herself. Caleb's dream wasn't her first. When she was a young child, she'd been cowering and terrorized in her nightmares. Her parents had taken her to a number of different psychologists, and one had suggested Mala try to control her dreams.

That had been the beginning of Mala taking charge.

At first it had been minor stuff. Mala receiving someone's fear and barely holding on to it before throwing it out at once—and making the monster blink. It had sometimes helped, not always. It hadn't been taking charge so much as trying to do *something*.

When she got older, she became more immune to the barrage of emotions, more able to keep her head so she could act. One dream had been the turning point. The fear had been so intense, so suffocating, and Mala had attempted to make the emotions smaller and more manageable. She'd ended up concentrating them, almost by accident. She hadn't shaped it properly, not like she could do now, but by the time she'd thrown it in the face of the blue-eyed wolf—she remembered that repeat offender—the force of it had been enough to knock him out.

And she thought, she hoped, that the female wolf had escaped from him.

A tear leaked down her cheek. In her nightmares, some of those wolves had died. This meant they had really, truly died. Having known their fear, that knowledge hurt and a kind of grief surrounded her. She'd grieved for them in the past—a part of her must have known the truth without today's proof—but back then she was able to insist to herself that it was only a dream.

It had never helped all that much.

She had tried to forget them, those lost wolves, and most of the deaths had occurred years ago when she'd been helpless and ineffective, but an ache settled in her chest.

Some time around three a.m., Mala dozed lightly, too cautious to go into a dream. She couldn't face that tonight after the revelation. She feared being sucked into some terror where she was incapable of saving someone's life.

Then there were the other times, the *many* times, when a beacon of fear had shown itself in her dreams and she'd been able to shut it down, choosing to avoid it, even forcing herself awake to escape the nightmare. But now, knowing it was real, knowing someone might be endangered and she could help them, it would be wrong not to investigate.

"Just not tonight," she whispered aloud.

By six thirty, she was up and showered, and the idea of pacing around the small room was insupportable. It was dark, but gray tinted the edge of the eastern sky, and so she went downstairs and outdoors.

Surely walking the streets at dawn wasn't dangerous.

The streets were quiet, though some people were moving about. It was a small town, she reminded herself, not Toronto with its early-morning bustle.

And it was *cold*. She wasn't going to last long, so she picked up the pace in the hopes that exercise would heat up her body, and strode forward.

It didn't take long to reach the end of town, though she wasn't as warm as she liked and she'd have to turn around soon. As she looked back, she saw a wolf behind her, following at a distance.

Her nightmares bore down on her, a claustrophobia of memories—being chased by a wolf or wolves—and despite common sense saying it was the wrong thing to do, she ran. Glancing behind her, she saw the wolf wasn't gaining. In fact, it had disappeared. She stuttered to a stop and turned in a slow circle on the empty road.

God, had the wolf been a figment of her imagination? She didn't think so, but she was a bit overwrought and hadn't slept well. She ran back towards town. It was stupid to try to escape a wolf by going *into* the wilderness. What she needed was a building, a closed door. She breathed easier once she neared the B and B. The sky was beginning to lighten. She shot a brief look over her shoulder only to see the wolf standing there again.

Crap. She raced forward, aiming for the B and B, it wasn't far, and almost slammed into Eden going through the front door.

Eden seized her arm, stabilizing her, and overcome, Mala bent down, hands on knees, breathing hard. She was in terrible shape. Of course, she hadn't known she'd have to outrun wolves before she'd arrived in Wolf Town, but being in shape had suddenly become an important priority.

"There there." Eden patted her back and sounded concerned. Was this the same woman as yesterday? "What happened?"

"A wolf," Mala gasped out. "It was chasing me."

After a few more pats and Mala having regained her breath to some degree, she pushed up to standing and looked into

Eden's face. Her scowl deepened, and Mala didn't think she could cope with Eden becoming offended and angry with her. However, the older woman turned away and opened her front door.

"Who's out there?" she demanded, like a schoolmarm preparing to chastise a misbehaving pupil.

Something, some*one*, barked.

"What do you think you're doing frightening her like that?" Eden's arm jerked up in a wide arc. "What is that supposed to accomplish?"

It, he, she—one of the above—whined, and Mala's near-escape from death no longer seemed to be quite that—more like a misunderstanding on her part.

Eden wagged a finger in the air, before using it to punctuate her words. "You're too handsome for your own good, you forget to use your brains. Get away and I'll look after her."

There was another noise, kind of a bark, kind of a protest, and Eden came back inside shaking her head. "Honestly. I think Jancis got all the brains when they were in utero."

Mala blinked. "The wolf is Jancis's twin?" No one had told her that was the relationship between Jancis and her brother, but Eden implied as much.

"Rory, yes. He was supposed to watch over you, make sure you were all right, not frighten you half to death." At Mala's look of disbelief, Eden added, "He's a big lug and doesn't always think things through. But he's good-hearted."

Big lug? Good-hearted? It was hard to reconcile these descriptions with her dreams. "I thought he was chasing me."

"Yes, well, you made that clear." Eden's expressions ranged from scowls to frowns to those of worry, and now it was the latter. What had happened to yesterday's Eden who hated her?

"You're shivering, dear. Get in here and drink something warm. This is a B and B, after all, and I serve breakfast."

Mala hadn't the energy to do anything but Eden's bidding, so she sat down with warm tea and porridge and scrambled eggs and ate them all. The cold, or something, had made her very hungry.

The phone rang, and Angus went from sleep to full awake as he picked it up.

"I've been kicked off duty," said Rory.

"Says who?" Angus scrubbed his face. Rory had been tasked with watching Mala until she arrived at his place. "What happened?"

"Mala went for a walk and I frightened her. She thought I was chasing her or something."

"Did you chase her?"

"No," Rory scoffed. "C'mon, Dad."

"Well, I'm wondering how she'd get that impression—"

"I *followed* her. But don't worry." Rory grunted softly, which didn't fit with the conversation. "Eden's got her. She's the one who booted me off Mala patrol. Thought you might want to go over."

Angus heard a rumble, as if Rory was holding in laughter. He sighed. "Can you two wait until I get off the phone?"

"Yes, we can wait," said Rory too loudly, the words clearly directed at his boyfriend. He cleared his throat. "Sorry, Dad. Mala's fine though. Eden went all mother hen on her, which is maybe good."

"Okay, okay, I get the picture. Talk to you later."

"Bye, Dad."

Angus pulled on his clothes. Eden was dependable, but she wasn't going to prevent Mala from leaving town. Fortunately the first bus didn't arrive until later in the morning. Still, he decided to make his way over to the B and B.

By the time he arrived, Eden was in her kitchen and Mala was nowhere to be seen. With one glance at him, Eden said, "She's in her room."

"How is she?"

"Looks like she didn't sleep last night."

"What?" He cocked his head, overplaying his question. "Why, Eden, is that concern I hear in your voice?"

She slid him a look, a hint of a smile with it. "Sure. I find it hard to see her as a threat when she's shaking in her boots just because Rory was down the road from her." She put the dishtowel down. "What is she doing here anyway, and how is she related to Caleb?"

"We don't exactly know."

"Uh-huh. You mean, it's best that *I* don't know," Eden said.

Angus shrugged in reply, an acknowledgment of Eden's statement. He wasn't going to get into dreams and wraiths and all that shit with her. Angus had gotten hold of Trey last night, and while Trey didn't dismiss what he'd been told—he was a cautious kind of guy—he'd said it was new to him.

"Worrying," Angus had replied to Trey's silence as he mulled over Angus's news.

"Well, more unusual abilities may come out of the woodwork, now that the world knows about shifters and Minders." Trey paused. "I'll dig deeper, without putting Caleb and Mala in danger."

"Thanks, Trey, I appreciate it." Angus had hung up and stared at the phone, wondering just what they were about to discover.

She'd meant to lie down for a few moments, recover from her scare followed by her breakfast feast. Eden's food had been surprisingly delicious. Or maybe not surprising. But given Eden's poisonous looks yesterday, Mala hadn't expected to enjoy her food.

But Mala began lightly dozing, where her thoughts were all over the place—wolves, Angus's blue eyes, Caleb's voice, cold wind across her face—and she made a point of keeping herself in limbo between wake and dream. She didn't want to go further into sleep. She didn't want to have a night terror away from home. That would have to wait until she reached her own bed, where it was safe to let go. Or as safe as it got.

Though she didn't know how long she could last without sleep. She refused to travel much for this exact reason.

The sleep pulled at her again. She'd resisted it enough that she sometimes felt that she and sleep were in a tug of war, a battle she usually didn't have much trouble winning, to be honest. She knew how to stay awake. But the last twenty-four hours had been an emotional drain and when she dozed deeper, she could no longer drag herself up and out of it. She tried to raise her internal alarm, the one that shook her awake with the warning to stay on guard. But the weariness blanketed her, softening her thoughts, and she tumbled into the darkness of sleep. She went deep.

It was hard to know how long she'd been out, but when the sky bleached to white, a precursor of a beacon, she became aware. Dreaming.

Not here, a part of her demanded, *not here*, though the reason wasn't entirely clear to her. The dreaming didn't listen, and the beacon, it called.

The beacon of fear. She'd spent years fighting its call and losing. And the stronger she'd become, the stronger the beacon's lure. Besides, now it was important, for reasons that eluded her at the moment. All she knew was she'd done important work recently. So she focused, aimed herself downward through white mist, through shapeless landscape, and jolted when she landed, anchored in...

...a wolf. Female.

Unusual. Her dreams were dominated by male wolves. She used to wonder if it had anything to do with being estranged from her father.

No time for thoughts of her father, of herself. There was immediate danger here. Occasionally she reached the fear before the danger was a full assault. Not today.

The female was cowering, ears back, teeth bared, furious and afraid. Mala hated coming in near the end like this, when it was so much harder to take control, to help. But at this juncture, there was no turning back.

The wolf jerked away from her attacker, barely aware of Mala who began fashioning her weapon, pulling the female's emotions to her, though the wolf didn't want to let them go. In her panic and her conviction she was going to die, it was all the she-wolf held on to.

Sometimes it was like that, but they hadn't much room to maneuver. The monster lunged and once again the female jumped backwards, out of the way.

She understood she was being played with, and Mala thought, *"Yes, let him play with you."*

Confusion raced through the female, her first awareness of her intruder. *"Friend,"* Mala assured her while she worked furiously, weaving in the anger, the fear, the terrible sorrow. The she-wolf wanted her life back, she wanted to never have

83

met her attacker.

Mala made her weapon strong, sharp. She knew how to forge fear into a harsh, bright jagged edge.

How had it come to this for the female wolf? *Not now, don't ask now.* Mala simply didn't have time. She pulled on the wolf's emotions, and after her initial resistance, the female released them to her, lacking the will to fight within, when the real danger bore down on her in the form of a large male wolf.

As she sharpened the brightness, Mala became more strongly aware of who this was—a female wolf older than her, terrified and angry. And far too alone.

"I'm here," Mala told her.

Unlike Caleb, the female didn't accept that Mala was something apart from her. She just gave in to the sensation of shedding the worst of her emotions so she could duck and weave while the monster nipped and bit her on this path where she'd been cornered, the morning light incongruously cheerful.

The she-wolf was bleeding. The pain made it difficult to focus.

In turn that made Mala angry and she wove her own emotion into the blade, once, twice, thrice. Then she looked up and out, through the she-wolf's eyes.

Into golden pupils. The eyes of a brown-furred wolf. Caleb's father.

He came at her then, and Mala thrust, no hesitation, letting her own anger feed her attack on him.

Upon entry, she felt his shock first, followed by fury and a recognition that this had happened to him before, even as he fought against her invasion, even as she anchored inside him. He couldn't believe this was happening once more, had thought the other instance a one-time aberration, and Mala could taste his rage, it was so strong within.

No one stops me. His thought, his declaration.

She didn't speak to him, hiding herself within the white blade that held his heart still as she worked deeper into the muscle, stopping its beat until he had no choice but to collapse to the ground.

I won't let go this time, she told herself.

Before today, these attacks had been all about her and her need to take control of the dream. But now she knew different. And while she didn't know if her dream blade could slay Caleb's father, she would stay here forever, if necessary. She wanted the she-wolf to go free.

"Who are you?"

Blearily, Mala tried to focus on where that thought came from. She couldn't look out through the eyes of Caleb's father because they had closed, his body shutting down. But he was still there, still aware—and aware of her.

The female who'd been cornered, who'd called Mala to her, was gone. She'd fled as soon as Caleb's father had stopped his attack, Mala had seen that much. The escape was good, but just as important was that Caleb's father be in no shape to follow her.

"You've been here before." It was a struggle, Mala recognized, for him to communicate with her. But it also indicated that Caleb's father was not dead, not even unconscious, no matter what he might look like to the outside world.

He wanted to know her, and she tried to stay hidden in the white shine of the blade.

"Time to leave."

He was right, she wanted to leave. Desperately. The old

panic clawed at her, the fear she would die in the body she'd attacked and never awake from the dream. He scented her fear.

"You will *die."* This pleased him and he used it as threat, but he didn't know what he was talking about. This was all new to him and he was guessing. She thought of Caleb and fought to hold on.

Surprise flowed through her and that surprise came from him. *"You know Caleb?"* he asked.

She went as still and small as possible. That feeling of being watched crawled through her consciousness, somewhat akin to when she'd boarded the bus in Toronto to travel north. She tried not to think, tried not to give things away. If staying longer and sharing her thoughts with this monster endangered Caleb, she would have to float free.

His thoughts were getting muddier, darker, in his effort to remain conscious. His energy was draining, because of her. *"I'm Caleb's father, John. Give me your name."*

She resisted his demand.

"Your name," he insisted, relishing her fear, despite his dire situation. For he was used to delivering commands, ultimatums. Used to getting his way. His will seemed to assail her. He was fighting for his life, and she did not want him to have it.

"Wraith, leave me now and I will forget you. Otherwise, I will know your name."

She blanked her mind, refusing to think it, yet it came anyway. "Mala."

But she had not said her name. She was hiding from it, hiding from the sound. Someone was betraying her identity.

Her world shook, her grip loosened. The blade began to slide out and her with it.

"Mala." This time more insistent. "Wake up." She absorbed sound.

"Yes, wake up, Mala."

Caleb's father's body strengthened, and he fought to push her out. Her world shook again and she could not stay within him. She slid out with the blade and rose above his body, *John's* body. As her world turned to white, she watched the monster breathe, eyes closed but body faintly stirring. All too soon, he would clamber to his feet yet again. She hoped the female wolf had enough time to flee to safety.

Chapter Eight

Angus had been prepared to wait for Mala to descend from her room. After all, he wanted to give her the impression he was her friendly host, not her jailer trying to keep her under lock and key in Wolf Town.

And he did wait, for over an hour. Then, as he sipped his second cup of coffee, a keening noise came from above. Yes, he had great hearing, he was a wolf, but that distressed sound carried far. The hair on the back of his neck rose.

His gaze rested on Eden's for a brief moment. "Get the key in case her door is locked."

He ran to the stairs, took them two at a time, and reached her room. Through the door, he heard smaller noises of distress. Once it sounded like a yip of pain.

Christ. What was going on? The door was locked, the lever stuck at horizontal with no give, and Angus considered breaking the door in. But Eden was on his heels, key in hand, so he moved aside and she slid the key into the lock and turned the handle down.

He barreled in to see Mala lying ramrod stiff on the bed, her body frozen with tension. She was breathing loudly, as if under duress.

Jesus. He went to her, unsure of what to do. He crouched beside the bed without touching her and murmured, "Mala."

She didn't respond, and carefully, not wanting to alarm her, he placed a hand on her shoulder. When she didn't react, just seemed lost to wherever her dreams had taken her, he put both hands on her shoulders and shook her gently.

Was it this way for her every time she slept? He couldn't imagine such a life.

"Mala, wake up," he urged.

She was gasping, and he backed away, worried he'd done more harm than good. Her body started to relax and, all of a sudden, she jackknifed to sitting, eyes wide open, stark terror on her face.

"Mala," he repeated a third time, and her chest heaved once, pulling in a long inhale. Again he reached for her, watching for her reaction, making sure his hand on her shoulder didn't alarm her further.

She accepted his touch and he slid his palm down her back as she caught her breath. He settled in beside her on the bed, eased an arm around her slim shoulders and drew her to him, and she allowed it all.

If she'd been a wolf, she might have leaned into him more, seeking more comfort in touch, but she didn't pull away, simply rested there, head against his chest.

He pushed hair off her sweaty brow and tilted her face up to look at him. "Tell me what happened."

Her eyes were wide and dilated. She blinked, seemingly mesmerized, and he wondered if she was able to answer. But she swallowed and spoke. "He's going to kill her."

Angus froze. *Dream wraith,* he reminded himself. Little understood, more the stuff of myth than reality. Until now. If he was right, she had witnessed something real, something he'd woken her from. He didn't know if his intervention was good or bad. But he feared it was the latter. "Where? Where is this happening?"

She shook her head, then appeared to recognize she was in a close embrace with Angus and stiffened up, pulled away. Rubbing her face hard, she looked disoriented. "I have no idea where. But it was *him*."

"Who?"

"In the dream, the attacker. It was Caleb's father." She sagged wearily, staring down at the bed's sheets. "Again. The worst ones always do reappear."

Angus looked away and closed his eyes.

Fucking hell.

She should have wanted to disappear. Talking about her nightmares had always been a disaster, in every way possible, so a part of her reflexively wanted to flee. But Angus was on the phone to someone named Trey, trying to locate where John Davies could be.

Angus was taking her dream very seriously.

"Did you get the woman's name?" Angus asked her, breaking from his talk with Trey.

"She didn't give it, she didn't think it." *No time*, Mala could have added.

Angus nodded, as if that made perfect sense, and waited to see if Mala had more to say.

"She was small, smaller than Caleb's father." In case it wasn't obvious, she added, "As a wolf."

"Hear that?" Angus said to the phone and Trey on the other end mumbled back while Angus nodded encouragingly at her. *Any details you can remember*, he'd said earlier before he'd called up Trey, *might be helpful*. The thought of her dreams being helpful to someone was dizzying, but she had to concentrate. She tried to remember back to that feeling of being inside the she-wolf.

"Maybe she was near Caleb's size. It felt about the same. Though it's hard to know if what I feel translates into...reality."

"What was around you? Snow?"

"No." The realization surprised her. "No snow. Not like here. It could have been near where Caleb was attacked by his father, the ground was similar, no longer icy though. But I didn't have a lot of time. I didn't focus on where I was. I didn't realize it was him until it was almost over." Right before she attacked.

Her voice had been rising at the end, and Angus's hand came down on her shoulder in reassurance. She wanted to lean into him, drape herself over him. It was a strange sensation, this desire to touch him, and it alarmed her.

"Just a sec, Trey." Angus placed the phone on the bed and crouched down to take Mala's cold hands in his warm palms, chafing them a little. He looked up at her, intent. "We're going to try to find the wolf who was being harmed, and I need to plan that. It might take a couple of hours for us to get everyone organized and prepared."

She nodded. The idea that people were acting on what she'd gleaned from her nightmare, she couldn't fathom it. Yet leaving that woman to be attacked again was plain wrong.

"Will you wait here?" Angus asked.

His sincerity, his concern for her, for everyone, undid her, and she could only say, "Yes."

"Please don't leave. We might need your help." He searched her face. "Can you stay longer?"

"Okay. I will." She put strength she didn't feel into the words, as a part of her yearned to go home after a nightmare and lick her wounds in private.

"Thank you, Mala." Then he did something lovely. He turned her palm upwards and kissed its center before he released her.

He stood and grabbed his phone. "Eden," he demanded. "Make sure Mala is comfortable and has whatever she needs. Charge everything to me."

Mala didn't have time to protest before Angus was out the door, talking once again on the phone, and she was left in her room to stare at Eden.

While Trey activated a handful of wolves who lived in southern Ontario, Angus enlisted nineteen from town. Together they would work a dragnet over the Niagara Peninsula. If they moved fast, they should be able to cover it effectively. For Angus, the most difficult thing about it was pulling Caleb out of school, both to talk about his father and to say he was going away for a few days.

Caleb's eyes had grown shiny with fear and his voice had shrunk to a whisper as he described where he'd been living when he was found by John Davies, but it confirmed the location Angus needed.

Not that there was any guarantee they'd find either Davies or the woman he was terrorizing. But they had to try.

Angus almost chose not to go himself. The situation was a little fragile, with Mala and her powers recently discovered and Caleb adjusting to his new life. Yet Angus had the best sense of smell of all in Wolf Town. It might make a difference in the search, make a difference to this unknown woman's life.

He handed over Caleb to Jancis's and Rory's care. Mala's situation was the more tricky one. She'd said she would stay, and had meant it, but he hadn't been forthcoming about the number of days he'd be away. He knew Eden would do her best to make her comfortable, but Jancis and Mala hadn't clicked.

Mala was the key to something big, and Angus feared that if this got out—the reason for their search, the source of their information—she might be endangered. He didn't want Mala going anywhere until the dust settled and he had a firmer grip on the consequences of someone having her abilities. However, in the meantime, he didn't want her kept under lock and key either. A lot of werewolves weren't as capable of diplomacy as he was. There was a reason he was in charge of Wolf Town.

He called over to Aileen's apartment, not surprised when she didn't answer. Even as human, she didn't pay much attention to the phone, and let's face it, Aileen would be in her wolf form. So Angus, all the while phoning up different wolves who were going to accompany him, stalked over to her apartment building and up the stairs to rap on her unlocked door three times before opening it himself.

To find Aileen rousing from her sleep, all dark fur and golden eyes.

"I need you to shift." He'd never known someone so at ease with just staying wolf who wasn't feral. And Aileen, despite her discomfort with her human, was in no way feral. "Then I need you to remain human and keep Mala, the woman you were watching last night, company until I return."

Aileen eyed him, a slight question on her wolf's face. It could have meant, *Why me?* Or, *How long?* Or, *Is this a trick to keep me out of my wolf body?*

She might have also wondered where he was going, but he didn't know what she was thinking because she couldn't speak as wolf. He explained further. One advantage of being the only one in the room capable of speech was that Aileen couldn't argue with him.

"I think Mala will be more comfortable in another woman's

company. Yours, to be specific."

Aileen didn't get that, he knew, since she was strong and clever, and the male wolves around were very protective of her. But she'd accepted female fear of strange males as common wisdom when it had come up in previous situations or conversations.

"I hope to be back in a matter of days," he continued. "And, this is important, *really* important. We need to convince Mala to stay with us in Wolf Town. We need to better understand what she's doing, because she is connected to us in some way that no one understands. I also want her kept safe. That's important to me, *personally.*"

Of course the other problem with being the only one capable of speech was that the words kept going to fill the silence, and sometimes you said more than you planned.

But Aileen acquiesced. She trotted over to butt her head against his hand, her way of telling him, *Okay.*

"Thanks, kiddo." He left then, that taken care of. Trey was already mobilizing his wolves, and Angus needed his group to get on the road.

At some point he or Trey would be obligated to contact their government liaison, but that would have to wait until the outcome of this search was known. Yes, they tried to be truthful with the official who was responsible for making the world's transition from mythical werewolves to real werewolves smooth and easy. But if Davies got ripped apart during this hunt, when he was already *persona non grata* in Canada, no wolf was going to give over information about the man's death. The cost was too high, and the specter of vicious, murderous werewolves wasn't going to help anyone, including humans.

Angus rubbed his forehead. Though neither he nor Trey had hesitated in forming this search party, there was a risk going all-out on this effort based solely on Mala's dream. Two questions kept coming round and round to him.

One, *was it actually real?* Because, as Trey pointed out, this could be all for naught and have nothing whatever to do with reality. Mala's dreams could be just that, despite Caleb's unusual reaction to her. But in case a life was now hanging in the balance, a life that could be saved, he and Trey had agreed to believe, for the interim, that what Mala had witnessed was real.

And two, if it was real, *had the female werewolf survived?* Mala was unclear on this point, and Angus had the awful feeling that he'd interrupted her trying to save the woman. Mala had been keening, rigid in body, terrorized, and he'd wanted to wake her from that horror.

But it appeared that he might have woken her from much more than a dream.

Mala had made a huge mistake. As she paced the small room, exhausted, overwrought and unable to sleep, she considered going back on her word. It had only been a few hours since Angus had asked if she would stay. But when she'd told him yes, she'd thought he meant another day or so.

Now Eden was talking as if Angus might be gone for an entire *week*, and he expected Mala to sit tight during that time. Meanwhile Eden assumed that Mala would do what Angus wanted, that everyone would do as Angus wanted.

Well, maybe in Wolf Town people did his bidding—he was alpha, whatever that really meant—but *she* didn't live in Wolf Town. She was her own person.

And she longed to sleep in her own bed. Not that she could even face sleep.

She sank onto the B and B's bed with something like

despair. Her logic was going out the window. She was no longer sure what she wanted, because while she longed for home, the idea of not seeing Angus again, or Caleb, was disturbing.

When she seriously considered packing up her small bag and walking out of here, two pictures came to mind. One of Angus kissing her palm—she couldn't get that gesture out of her head and was giving it way too much significance. But more, she thought of young Caleb. There was a shared experience between them and she wanted to see him again.

And to be honest with herself, she wanted to know the outcome of Angus's search for the woman in her dreams. Mala wouldn't be leaving and she knew it, even while she chafed at being stuck in a small town in northern Ontario.

Maybe she needed to go for a walk to get rid of this claustrophobic feeling. Problem was she liked to hide away after a bad dream, not venture out into the open where she felt more vulnerable.

A knock came at the door and Mala sighed inwardly. That would be Eden who, despite her abrupt ways, had checked in on Mala about once an hour since Angus had left. Though sorely tempted, Mala didn't think she could yell through the door, *Don't worry! I haven't collapsed yet.*

Instead she said, "Come in."

The door edged open, more slowly than Eden who tended to sail in as though she belonged in her own B and B. Once the door was fully open, Mala stared at a young woman, somewhat taller than her, with short dark hair and the most amazing golden eyes.

Eerily similar to John Davies's eyes, Mala realized with some shock, and she pushed to standing.

But this was no attacking wolf. The girl looked uncertain, given Mala's jumpy reaction, and at that, Caleb's father was no longer anywhere in the girl's face, which was open and kind. So unlike his cruelty.

Her clothes were loose, and despite her age she didn't look like a teenager. She seemed young but...untethered. If that made any sense whatsoever.

She shifted her weight, not quite hopping from foot to foot, and her expression turned almost bashful. "I'm Aileen."

"Hello," said Mala, for wont of anything else to say. She shook her head, trying for the proper response. "I'm Mala."

"Angus asked me to say hello."

"Oh." *Why would he do that?* But Mala bit her tongue. It might sound rude and she found she didn't want to be rude to this girl.

"Can I come in? Or would you rather come downstairs and eat something? Lunch is being served."

"Uh..." Mala didn't want to make conversation, but Aileen bit her lip as if she was about to be rejected, so Mala smiled and said, "I'll come downstairs."

The girl smiled back brilliantly. "Thanks."

Thanks? Mala mentally shrugged and grabbed her purse. It wouldn't do her any harm to eat—or push food around her plate if she couldn't find her appetite. After all, Angus was paying for everything. Eden had reassured Mala on this point more than once, though Mala had grasped the concept the first time. In fact, her initial reaction had been to argue, but that would be a futile, empty gesture and nothing more, given she couldn't afford to stay here for a week.

When they entered the restaurant, Eden hustled over, pleased to see them both, completely different from when Mala had first arrived in Wolf Town. Had that only been yesterday morning?

"Aileen!" Eden enveloped her in a big hug, then stepped back, as if they hadn't seen each other for ages. She had the type of expression worn by older women who declared to a gangly teenager that they'd grown. Not that Eden said those words.

"I'm here," exclaimed Aileen happily, lifting her arms out from her body before letting them fall back to her sides.

"Sit down, sit down." Eden led the way to an empty table. "Figure out what you want. I know you must be hungry."

As they seated themselves, Mala looked at Aileen in question. "Have you been away?"

"Oh no." Her tone suggested that idea was ridiculous. "I hardly ever leave Wolf Town. It's my home. I love it here." At Mala's frown, she asked, "Why?"

"It seemed like Eden hasn't seen you for a while."

"She hasn't." Aileen picked up the menu to hide behind, before putting it down to blurt out her explanation. "I stay wolf too much. I haven't been human for a while. That's why Eden's glad to see me."

"Oh." Mala was fascinated despite herself. "How long has it been since Eden saw you..." she rolled her hand in her search for the right words, "...like this?"

Aileen looked around for guidance of some sort. "What's the date?"

"March thirteenth."

Aileen pulled a face. "More than a month. Oops." At first she seemed amused by this realization but then she glanced at Mala, expecting censure, perhaps. "I'm a bit of a freak, I'm afraid."

Mala burst out laughing before covering her mouth with her fist. She hadn't meant to make that noise and feared she'd offended Aileen. "*I* am the freak."

"Oh yeah?" Aileen went back to the menu, before glancing up again. "Then you should stay in Wolf Town with me."

Her smile was adorable. This lunch reminded Mala of when she was young, and she and her cousins used to hang out like sisters.

Whoa. Don't be ridiculous. You just met this girl.

Aileen slapped the plastic menu down on the table. "Ready to eat? I'm starving."

Mala nodded, having picked out a sandwich.

Eden came over right away, turning to Mala first, who gave her order. Next Aileen asked for a hamburger, a pizza and some pasta. Mala blinked, and Aileen grinned again. "*Really* starving."

Chapter Nine

In four vehicles, they drove for ten hours, mostly due south, with a slight curve around Lake Ontario to reach the Niagara Peninsula. They traveled through the afternoon and into the night, arriving near midnight to rendezvous with Trey and his people.

The address was a house belonging to a she-wolf and her human husband. Veronica was about the tenth female werewolf Angus had met, which went to show how rare they could be. He made a mental note to get Aileen to meet Veronica in person. He sometimes thought the reason Aileen remained uncomfortable in her human skin was because of a lack of female mentors.

But now was not the time. They were on a search for, he hoped, the eleventh she-wolf he would come to know. Trey had done some homework, had established six areas that would be swept. They would divide into groups of five or six wolves then separate, planning to regroup forty-eight hours later.

"I'm taking…" Angus stabbed his finger at one-sixth of the area they would cover, the one that included Welland, Caleb's former place of residence before his father had flushed him out.

Trey glanced at him. "You think you can find her there?"

While Angus believed in the power of aiming high, he had his reservations. He shrugged. "I may have the best chance."

"All right, I want Veronica to go with you." Trey beckoned

his niece over, and Angus observed that her husband bristled. Trey shot him a look. "This isn't dangerous, David."

"Yeah," the blond man drawled. "Just a psycho wolf out there terrorizing women and children."

"We're going in pairs," Trey pointed out calmly, "and John Davies seems to work solo."

"*Seems*," her husband repeated.

"David," Veronica protested, and their eyes locked.

Some kind of silent communication went on between the married couple, and David's face softened into a grudging smile. "You kick his ass, honey."

"Exactly," she said.

After that, logistics were gone through, where each group would fan out from and where they'd meet up to assess their progress. Contact numbers were exchanged. Then they broke up into their respective groups and piled into their vehicles.

They had another hour and a half drive through the middle of the night, and Angus barely spoke further. Veronica wanted to sleep to keep up her energy, and the four other men were either doing the same or weren't much for talking. At three in the morning, the six of them climbed out of the van, stripped off their clothing and shifted.

It was a forced shift, not like under the full moon when they were ready to run, but it still felt right, being called by the need to track down an unknown endangered female wolf and her assailant. Because female wolves were so rare, there was a real drive within himself and others to keep them safe.

Angus came back to awareness first. His bones ached, his muscles had tensed up, but he was standing and shaking himself out, trying to get comfortable in his wolf skin when the moon shone at a quarter of its size.

He stood watch as the others regained consciousness in their wolf forms. Veronica was the third to rise on all fours, and he scented sharp fear, normal for a female among strange males. He rumbled reassurance and their gazes met, hers golden under the thin moonlight.

She gave back a muted whine then trotted off a small distance. Once they were all on their feet, the two other pairs headed off and Angus paced over to Veronica. Together, they began to lope, a steady gait that they could keep up for some distance. It was odd for Angus to run with this she-wolf who was around his age, and a strange ache lodged itself in his chest.

Though he'd had different lovers over the years, he'd always longed for a female companion. He'd carried this idea he needed a wolf to be his, but they were rare, and even then, rarely available. The chance of hitting it off was remote, were he to meet one who was single, he understood that. And he entertained no hopes of such a connection with the she-wolf they searched for. She'd be traumatized.

Also, and it was strange to admit, tonight his thoughts kept circling back to Mala.

He'd always been too wolf-focused. When his son had taken up with a non-wolf this past year, Angus had assumed it wouldn't be serious, that it would be short-lived—for many reasons, but partly, yes, because Scott was not a shifter. Angus had been wrong. It had been, in the end, quite wonderful to watch Rory grow as he settled into a relationship with someone who wasn't trying to court the alpha's son, curry favor with the ruling family as it were. Someone who didn't really comprehend the concept of the alpha's son and who simply wanted Rory for himself.

But Angus, well, he found it hard to put his guard down

among non-wolves. The cloak of secrecy he'd grown up with was difficult to relinquish. Yet Veronica had done so with her husband.

She barked, and he pulled his head out of his ass and concentrated on the hunt. The first scent they followed was that of a coyote—their population was rising in southern Ontario. Next they discovered human teens out late at night near a small suburb, some falling-down drunk, which made Angus sigh, even as he acknowledged that it wasn't only werewolf teens who acted out.

The dawn came and went, and Veronica's pace didn't flag. Angus could tell she was invested in this hunt, worried about the woman, even if they couldn't truly know the she-wolf existed. Their work was trickier during the day, given they had to keep out of sight of humans, but they continued their sweep of the area, occasionally investigating odd scents and smells, even if they didn't indicate a werewolf had been in the area.

It wasn't until late evening that they stumbled upon something that brought Angus up short. Veronica, her gold eyes visible in the darkness, looked at him in question while Angus opened his mouth and breathed, taking in as much of the scent as possible.

Caleb, but not Caleb.

Wolves' scents resembled each other when they were related, and this scent in the air was too close to that of Caleb's to ignore. It was family, and likely his father, John. Faint, but Angus didn't get these things wrong. He tracked the werewolf out of the conservation area and into a suburb.

Quietly, Veronica followed, understanding he'd picked up the trail of a werewolf, if not knowing who. When they came to the house, Angus made the decision to shift. He disliked shifting in such conditions—in front of someone he didn't know well and near human civilization. But time was at a premium.

He turned and met Veronica's gaze, and she gave the slightest of nods. Then he focused inwards, looking for his human who didn't want to come out under these circumstances. He had to remind himself of the woman who needed to be found before it was too late. He thought of pulling back his wolf skin, an almost violent motion imagined, and there it was before him. The shift in presence, the wolf receding, his world receding, as the blackness surrounded him and turned him inside out.

When he came to, lying on his side on the rough ground, he swore. What the hell had his wolf been thinking? It was freezing, and he was fucking naked in early spring. He was not going to be able to suss out information on Davies or the woman by knocking on the front doors of strangers while he stood nude on the doorstep. They'd simply call the police on the creepy streaker, and wouldn't that be fun?

Veronica gave a low woof, so Angus rolled into a crouch and then rose, following her. It took about ten minutes, but Veronica identified a quiet house, her sense of hearing now better than his, given their different forms.

The house was empty of people though not uninhabited. While the heat from the shift still kept Angus warm, that wouldn't last forever and he needed clothes. The back door was locked, no surprise, but it was a cheap knob rather than a deadlock, and it didn't take much strength to break it. He paused a moment as he entered the house, listening for the sound of a house alarm going off. When none came, he strolled through the rooms, hoping to find clothes that would fit him, and discovered the master bedroom.

The man of the house was shorter but heavier than him, so Angus belted himself into a pair of jeans that came down to mid-calf. The shirt wasn't as bad a fit. The winter jacket was fine.

As he stepped out of the house again, Veronica sat there and leveled him a wolfish grin, her first, and he smiled as he looked down at his too-short jeans. "They call these capris, right?"

Then they sobered and marched over to the house which held Davies's scent, though said scent indicated Davies had been here days ago. Angus directed Veronica to hide back in the woods, and she balked at the idea of retreating.

"There's little you can do," he argued. "And if things go south, I absolutely need you to get back to the others. For *her* sake."

Veronica came up to him, licked his hand in a token of good luck and trotted off towards the woods.

"If I'm not back in an hour, go," he called after her.

Veronica paid him no mind though she'd heard him. He turned towards the suburb. While sneaking in the back door of someone's home was an option, he chose to walk up to the front doorstep and ring the bell.

It took more than a few minutes, but a woman who he'd roused from sleep answered the door, opening it to a strange man. Unwise, even reckless. He breathed in—she was human—and with a quirk of her mouth she acknowledged his scenting her.

Her smile came slowly, just this side of inviting. "Are you a friend of John's?"

So, she'd identified him as wolf. That was okay.

"Not exactly," he prevaricated, unwilling to say yes to her question. "I need to find him and I gather he's been around recently."

She glanced down at his high-water pants. "You guys wear the most interesting outfits sometimes," she deadpanned. "Would you like to come in?"

He paused. He wanted answers, not a social call, but he wasn't going to get one without the other. She desired his company and he needed to play that game, without raising false hopes, in case he required more information from her down the road. Still, something in him resisted going inside, playing human when he wanted to hunt as wolf.

"We can talk over tea," she suggested.

"Is something going on here?"

She blinked at his brusque tone. "I thought you could tell me."

Okay, perhaps tea would be best, sort this out. "I'm afraid I don't have a lot of time."

"You guys never do."

We're not all the same, lady. But he kept that thought to himself as he stepped inside. Again he breathed the air, guessing John had been here two or three days ago—before Mala's dream of yesterday morning.

Mala. He'd left her in the care of his people, yet Angus pushed down the urge to make a phone call and repeat to them the overwhelming importance of keeping this newly found dream wraith safe.

If people discovered what she could do—if she'd actually done it, Angus reminded himself, though he didn't take his doubts on this score seriously—she would be a target. No question.

The woman threw cold cuts on the table and Angus wasn't shy about eating them. She knew her wolves and their need to eat, evidently, and he'd just shifted, would shift again soon.

"So, are you also looking for Sally?" she asked.

He held her gaze, made a point of not looking confused. His gut screamed that this was very important, and the too-casual way she'd flipped the question at him suggested the woman before him was jealous.

"What's your name?" he asked.

"Pamela."

"Pamela. I'm Angus."

"That's a nice old-fashioned name."

"Thank you." He gave an ironic tip of the head towards her. When she passed him a mug, he cradled it in his hands, though he wasn't a big tea drinker. "Pamela, tell me why you're asking me about Sally."

A resentment built in her eyes. Not murderous, this was lower-level emotion, some hurt, some annoyance. And jealousy. Sometimes that led to lies, so he had to be careful.

"Please," he added, and she responded to his plea.

"John." She shook her head, then laughed at herself. "He's left me for Sally, if you must know. Though maybe you already do."

"I didn't know," Angus said mildly.

"We were together for six months, which isn't long. I realize that. But..." she lifted one shoulder, "...I thought he was more serious than to just...drop me."

Lady, if he's left you, you don't know how lucky you are. He stomped down on his urge to give her a lecture then and there about safety. Because she shouldn't have invited him into her house.

"John called me a groupie."

Angus nodded for her to continue.

"Sure, I like wolves." Her gaze focused on Angus. "I could like you. But I still thought John and I were going somewhere. I thought we had a connection."

Angus wondered if she'd been hoping for a mate. There were sometimes rumors among the humans that if they could get a wolf to be their mate, they'd live longer, have better sex, make super children. He wondered who the fuck had started that bullshit. No one lived longer, the sex, like any other couple, depended on the couple themselves, and the children were either human or werewolf, like their parents.

"You seem like a nice woman, Pamela, so I'm going to be straight with you."

She pulled back her shoulders, bracing herself, and looked him straight in the eye.

"From what I know of John, he's unlikely to ever settle down. Don't blame this on yourself."

"Don't patronize me." With a roll of her eyes, more self-deprecating than rude, she asked, "What do you want of John?"

"Family matters, I'm afraid. Can you tell me where he is?"

She spread her hands out to indicate her helplessness. "He sure didn't leave me a forwarding address."

"Sally, then, can you tell me where she is?"

Pamela paused, trying to figure out the meaning behind his questions. "She's a wolf, isn't she? That's why he dropped me."

Angus suspected Sally was the she-wolf they were looking for. He also suspected Sally wasn't interested in John, hence his violence. Some males liked to control a female wolf, and John was likely one of them. Whether a female wolf wanted to be anywhere near him didn't matter once they'd been found. "Perhaps. But I don't yet know. That's why I need your help. I don't have enough information. If you can tell me where Sally is, I'd be grateful."

She crossed her arms. "If I help you, get John to visit me one more time."

Angus could see what she wanted. One last chance to seduce John, convince him to come back to her. It was written in her body's posture.

He didn't think lying was going to work with this woman. She was observant. Besides, lies didn't come easily to him. "John's a shit, Pamela. I'd be doing you no favors convincing him of that, and to be quite frank, I have no reason to think he'd listen to me on this." Or anything else for that matter.

After regarding him for a moment, she rose and poured her untouched tea into the sink. "You're honest with me. I'll give you that much."

He waited and she sighed.

"Sally lives in the very small town of Flint Hill. It's about a two-hour drive from here."

Crap.

Something in his face must have given him away, because Pamela looked a little worried. "I hate her, but I don't wish her harm. Is she in trouble?"

"Did John never beat you?"

Pamela shook her head. "I don't put up with that. Did he...?" She frowned, disbelief clear on her face. "Are you claiming he's beaten others?"

Angus was thinking of Caleb but he wasn't going to mention John's son. "Yes, I am claiming that."

She blinked once, not convinced, but willing to consider the possibility.

He stood abruptly. "I can't stay. Would you mind if I used your phone?"

She gestured to the landline. "Be my guest."

Angus picked it up and called Veronica's husband. David was playing central station when it came to messages from the wolves out on the search. Angus kept it brief, wording it in such a way that he didn't pass on information to Pamela, who made no pretense about giving him privacy and not eavesdropping. She didn't need to know about their comprehensive search for a she-wolf and Davies.

While Angus wanted to jump in a car and drive to Flint Hill, he had a job to finish here—and Sally could be a red herring. He and Veronica needed to continue their sweep of their area while David passed on his information to the crew that was sweeping Flint Hill.

He bid goodbye to Pamela, brusque but not rude.

"Angus," she said as he walked down the front steps. She was hanging on to the door, embracing the freezing night.

Despite his impatience to get going, he turned back.

"John doesn't like other wolves very much." She bit her lip. "So you watch yourself."

He was glad John had dropped this woman—for her sake. "Thank you for that warning. But you do the same—watch yourself. And stay away from him."

Pamela smiled, as if she knew better. He didn't have the time, or even the ability to convince her otherwise, not now anyway. So Angus slipped into shadow.

Chapter Ten

After phoning his new information in, Angus and Veronica diligently continued their sweep, though he was anxious to be finished. But someone would have located Sally's home address. Another group was there, doing their job, and he would stay here and do his. Before he shifted back to wolf, he'd given Veronica a brief rundown on what he'd learned from Pamela.

They didn't find anything further, neither a second taste of Davies in the air, nor the scent of another werewolf, male or female. By the end of day two, the six of them met back at the van and, some as human, some as wolf, drove back to David and Veronica's.

Veronica hadn't shifted, which surprised Angus. He'd expected her to be human when she reunited with her husband. But she was tired, he expected, and once they got to her house and her husband opened their front door, she simply trotted up to where David was waiting and went into his open arms, leaning into him.

No discomfort in that embrace.

They waited on two more carloads to arrive, and for everyone to shift back to human in the privacy of a room, before they assembled in the crowded living area to get down to business.

Trey was running this, but he didn't blink when Angus almost pounced on the group who had covered Flint Hill. "Was she there?"

One of the men leaned forward, face weary, and shook his head.

"Nothing?" persisted Angus, figuring that at least they hadn't found her dead body. Death's scent was strong and hard to hide from werewolves.

"We figure she might have been home ten days ago or so. We broke in. It looked like she left in a rush. Dishes on the counter, laptop computer left open."

After that, Trey took over and they all gave reports that didn't amount to much of anything, even if it appeared everyone had been thorough. Angus and Veronica had found the most, but it wasn't enough, not nearly enough.

As the meeting was winding down, Trey looked across the room at Angus. "This may have been absolutely nothing, you know."

"Possible," Angus allowed. "But I don't think so. Not after talking to Pamela."

"We need more."

Angus held Trey's gaze, comprehending exactly what Trey meant. Angus had hoped it wouldn't come to this, had tried to ignore it as a possibility. For one thing, there was no telling if it would be a useful exercise in any way. And yet, they had to try. Or, to be more specific, Mala had to try. He had to ask her to dream.

Trey stood up. "Phone your wraith. See if she can find out more."

My wraith. He liked the territorial sound of that, if not what he'd been called upon to do.

Angus could have argued, could have made the point that Mala seemed to have little to no control over where she went in her dreams. She was a neophyte with no training in her abilities, nothing like those myths of powerful beings who ruled through their dreams.

But Angus didn't waste words and time. He picked up his phone.

Mala was exhausted. She should have found Aileen's constant company more aggravating, with all her eager and at times awkward questions, but Aileen was the most wide-eyed naïf Mala had yet to meet. Ironic since Mala sure didn't consider herself worldly and experienced, despite Aileen's attitude towards her. Mala tended towards the life of a hermit, even while living in Toronto.

"I wonder if I should visit Toronto some day," Aileen mused, as if she were considering a trip to Saturn's outer rings, a physically impossible trip but something to imagine on occasion when feeling your most outlandish.

She was in Mala's room, crouched down on the floor in this way she liked to sit. Aileen claimed she didn't find chairs comfortable, and in the three days they'd *hung out*, as Aileen described it, Mala was getting used to Aileen's way of making herself at ease.

"Are you inviting yourself to my place?" Mala asked with a smile. She rarely had people over, but given that Aileen knew more of her secrets than anyone in Toronto, the thought of having an out-of-town visitor was not unappealing.

Aileen tilted her head. "Okay."

"Okay," Mala echoed.

"After Angus gets back," Aileen amended, resting her head on her knees.

Mala nodded. Mustn't forget Angus, no one else in this bloody town did. Then again, neither did Mala. She worried that she was developing a crush on him. Why this infatuation would grow in his absence, she didn't know. Perhaps because he'd been the first person to take her dreams seriously. It was hard to resist that, and she was confusing this revelation with other feelings.

Aileen stared at her, her golden gaze seeing too much, because she said, "Don't worry. Angus likes you."

Mala snorted inelegantly. "Why do you say that?"

"I can tell by the way he talks about a person."

She didn't know how to respond to such a statement, so she didn't, though she hugged close the thought of Angus liking her. The rap that came at the door jolted her out of her nice thoughts. It was Eden's proprietary knock and Mala called, "Come in."

Eden entered, hand extended to pass something over to Mala, a cell phone.

"What?" asked Mala, not wanting to take it. If it was bad news, she'd rather Eden told her in person.

"Angus wants to talk to you."

"About what?" persisted Mala.

"I don't know," replied Eden slowly, like Mala was being dimwitted. "He didn't tell me, because it's *you* he wants to speak to."

Mala pulled in a breath and took the phone from Eden's hand. Despite it being so necessary he talk to her, it wasn't like Aileen and Eden were going to give her privacy either. Everyone loved to listen to what everyone said around here.

Or perhaps Mala simply wasn't used to being around people outside of work.

"Hello?" she asked.

"Mala." The way he said her name made her feel...important. Special. That said, his tone was solemn and his next words almost ominous. "I need you to do something for me."

It was on the tip of her tongue to say, *Anything.* But she would sound too eager. Besides, who knew what he wanted? She sure didn't. Unless... Her stomach dropped.

After all, he took her dreams seriously.

"We didn't find her, the wolf in your dream, but even apart from you, we have reason to think she's down here somewhere." He waited, as if he wanted her to say something but she resisted. "Can you try to find her in your dreams again?"

She always waited days before she slept after a nightmare. From a young age she'd learned that nightmares could return with the same horrifying monsters if she slept again too soon. She'd thought—once she'd been old enough to think in these terms—that she'd needed psychological distance in order not to revert to the recent nightmare. But the real explanation was more sinister, that whoever she'd dreamed of once was more likely to still be in danger, and that's why the night terrors recurred.

"Mala." This time his tone was insistent. Not commanding, not pleading. More of a *this has to done, will you help?* tone.

And it did have to be done, didn't it? If this woman was in danger from Caleb's asshole of a father, Mala needed to at least *try* to save her. She smoothed a damp hand across her jeans. She feared doing it, and she feared failing. "I've never dreamed on purpose before."

"I know."

"I don't know if I *can* do it. Or if it will help."

"I know that too. All I'm asking is that you make the attempt. That's all anyone can ask." He paused. "We think her name is Sally."

The name clinched it for Mala, made the danger to this woman more real. She glanced at Aileen and Eden who watched her. What if *they* were about to be harmed? Wouldn't Mala make the effort then? "No one can wake me up this time."

"I'm sorry I interfered with your previous dream. That was wrong of me."

A part of Mala was relieved. She'd been awake for too many days and she was exhausted. She would rest before she dreamed. It worked like that for her; she couldn't change it. After so much time awake, she couldn't go into a dream until she slept deeply.

Another part of Mala was curious. Yes, this wasn't something she would have ever asked for, deliberately being frightened out of her wits. But if she was going to continue to live through these nightmares, she preferred there be a purpose to them. She wanted to learn whether or not she *could* find someone.

"I'll do it," she told Angus. "I'll do it now. Truth is, I'm ready to fall over from sleep deprivation anyway."

"Thank you, Mala. I owe you."

The sincerity in his voice shook her. She didn't know why she was so affected by him. "It will take me a while," she warned. "I may sleep hours before I dream. I can't prevent that."

"You do whatever works." His tone warmed even further, making her shiver slightly. "You're a good person."

Mala huffed a laugh.

"Hand the phone back to Eden, okay? She'll be able to get in contact with me after you wake up."

"Good night." It sounded odd saying it, under the circumstances.

"You take care of yourself," Angus replied, and Mala passed the phone to Eden.

Aileen rose from her crouch and, making no effort to indicate she hadn't heard every word in that phone conversation, announced, "I am going to watch over you."

Mala scrubbed her eyes. The idea of Aileen standing beside her bed while she slept was intolerable, but she chose her words, not wanting to offend her new friend. "I need to be alone to sleep or it won't work. And no one can wake me up."

She observed Eden finish her conversation with Angus and drop the phone in her pocket. "Aileen, you take the room next door. Mala, if it sounds like you're in danger, we'll have to do something but we'll try to stay hands-off."

In danger? "You don't understand. I live alone. In a basement. So I don't disturb roommates when I dream. Nothing ever happens to me in those dreams. I always wake up in one piece." She couldn't stand the idea of being taken away from Sally at the worst possible moment. "You cannot wake me up. Please."

Solemn-faced, Eden nodded. "All right. We understand."

"I'm on my own here," Mala insisted.

"I'll sleep next door." Aileen pointed to the room one over. "I'll let people know if you're awake or still sleeping." In case Mala had forgotten, Aileen added, "My hearing is very good."

Since Mala couldn't see a way to object to that plan, she gave in. Then Eden was fussing about her eating enough and having clean towels, while Aileen got settled in her own room for the night.

By the time Mala was by herself in her room, it was past

midnight. She'd expected to fall asleep easily, being so tired, but her brain wouldn't turn off. Plus she worried that she would fail, be incapable of finding the she-wolf again. Self-direction in entering her dreams was a new concept, something she'd yet to practice. At least when it came to locating people. She did make choices once she was inside the nightmare.

Mala tried to find that idea encouraging.

She shied away from the idea that the woman might already be dead. *Her name is Sally,* Mala repeated to herself, as if the name itself would help find Sally in the dreams.

One moment Mala lay wide awake, forcing her eyes closed in a parody of sleep. The next, exhaustion flowed in like a wave and she let it take her down.

She went deep and for hours she knew nothing, her mind and body catching up on her dreamless sleep. But eventually she rose from those depths, and as she was rising, a part of her became alert to possibility.

She'd been here so often, in that limbo. Normally she fought to escape her dreams, until their lure became too strong for her to resist. But this time it was different, odd. She was searching.

Most of her life had been spent trying to avoid this horizon, trying to skim by without being taken prisoner by its forceful pull, and only being dragged along to a beacon when the attraction was so strong she could not resist its call. Now she wanted to explore the dreamworld.

The attraction being someone else's fear, which acted like a magnet calling to her...to her powers, she supposed.

There was no magnet here today. It would have been easy to rise and to wake. But she stayed in this in-between place, floating, searching for anything of significance. Not easy to find what had in the past always been obvious. It took a while for

118

her to observe that the landscape wasn't clear white but shifting towards color, and there was a shape in the distance that resonated with her. Not really a magnet, but something that called to her.

Caleb had been safe after the first nightmare, she reminded herself, and she'd found him then because the echo of his fear had been strong. This woman might have better control, better ways to keep herself hidden, but Mala would investigate. She let herself be pulled along towards meaning.

The way cleared, white turning to fog turning to the real world—and a woman, *the* woman, materialized as Mala joined her. She was crouched down, her back against the wall, just breathing, like that used up all her energy. Mala took anchor so she could stay. Without the immediate fear and terror, it would be easy to float off and away, rising up to consciousness.

She was reluctant to make her presence known, as if that would push the woman—it was the same woman, Mala felt the recognition—over the edge. So Mala assessed, sitting with her for long minutes as she did little but absorb the woman's despair.

From time to time the woman wiped her face, though there weren't tears exactly, and she whispered to herself, "It worked. It did."

Mala couldn't put it off any longer. She tried to make contact, using the name she had been given.

"Sally?"

The woman jolted, looked around despite sensing that Mala's voice had come from within her. Questions rose in Sally—*what, how, why?* But it was better not to offer explanations.

"Where are you?" Mala asked while trying to project calm.

Sally slowly shook her head, and Mala looked out through

119

her eyes to observe the surroundings. They seemed to be in a small laundry room, and while smell was not a sense that much made itself known to Mala in her dreams, the scent of bleach and lemon was overwhelming.

Sally sagged against the wall and thought, not really at Mala but it was easy to catch, *"I'm actually going crazy now."*

"No." Mala paused, unsure how to be convincing. *"Let me help you."*

"Sure. I can't afford to be fussy." There was a wry note that Mala found encouraging. *"I'd take help from anyone, even myself. If it was real."*

"Where are you?" she repeated.

After a moment of deciding that she couldn't do herself harm by telling herself where she was, Sally thought, *"An empty house. Starving to death, because if I go out he'll scent me. Why do you ask?"*

"I'm going to give you a number. You'll remember it and you'll phone out."

"I have no phone."

Mala gave her the number anyway, Angus's cell, made Sally repeat it, and Sally went along because she was frightened and bored out of her mind at the same time. Even if she believed this conversation signaled her imminent breakdown.

"Angus. You ask for Angus."

Tiredly, Sally nodded.

"What city or town are you in?"

"Flint Hill." This spoken aloud, with Sally sounding a touch annoyed. She pressed hands against her temples. "Now, go away."

"I'm going. Wait three hours, then get out and make the phone call."

120

Sally smiled and it was bitter. "John is going to kill me. I know he is."

Mala repeated the numbers, repeated Angus's name, while Sally tried to ignore her. Mala could feel her anchor in Sally losing strength, given the way Sally wanted to push her out, combined with Mala's body's own need to wake up. *"I have to go, Sally."*

Sally's voice was all weariness. "It's better that you do."

But despite wanting to leave immediately, wanting to warn Angus, Mala found herself in a state of inertia, hovering in Sally, unable to move off.

She sighed and drew some of Sally's fear towards her.

"What's going on?" Sally asked out loud, but Mala didn't answer, simply used that energy to swing herself out of Sally's body and into the light.

Chapter Eleven

It was difficult to wake up and Mala felt like she was scraping her way back to consciousness. She didn't know how long it took before she could open her eyes, and even then, she wasn't quite sure if she was really opening her eyes or dreaming of doing so.

But she wasn't in that laundry room with its sharp, toxic smell of bleach. It was the B and B, in the room she had rented from Eden—small, tidy, homey.

Weakly, she pushed herself up to sitting, then slapped the wall that stood between her room and Aileen's.

Seconds later, someone knocked and Mala said, "Come in."

Aileen crossed the room to take Mala's hands, which was sweet. "Are you okay?"

She nodded. "Sally wasn't being terrorized right then. She was alone. But very frightened."

Aileen's eyes widened and her hold on Mala's hands tightened. "You succeeded? You found her?"

Through her dry throat, Mala said, "I have to talk to Angus. Right away."

"I have Eden's cell." Aileen hit a button, presumably the one that dialed Angus, and handed the phone to Mala.

While she listened to it ring once, Aileen sprang from the

bed to the doorway to bellow, "Mala's awake, she's calling Angus."

"Hello," came Angus's voice in her ear. Mala gripped the cell tight, momentarily tongue-tied, unable to tell him what had happened. Describing her dreams in the past had always been disastrous.

Focus, Mala. This wasn't the past. This was Angus who knew so much about her, about wolves, about dreaming.

"Eden?" Angus asked into the silence, concern in his voice.

She pulled in a breath and got control of herself. "It's me, Mala, and I found her. Sally is in Flint Hill. Hiding in what looked like a laundry room of an empty house." Mala wasn't sure what that meant, hadn't thought to ask at the time. Was it on-sale empty? Or no-one-was-in-the-house empty? "The room smelled of bleach and lemon. She's frightened of John."

"She's trying to conceal her scent."

"Does that work?"

"Not for me."

"I gave her your number."

"You can do that?"

"Apparently. Or, I think I did that." Mala was waiting for this all to crash down and her to be consigned to the crazy bin. At the same time, the rush to find this woman before it was too late felt very, very real. "Get to Flint Hill. If she comes out of hiding to phone you, then you can reach her before John does. I told her three hours, though I don't know if she'll call. She thinks John is going to kill her."

"You've done good, Mala," Angus said.

At the compliment, warmth flowed through her. She nodded, unable to speak for that moment, then she heard a dial tone. He was gone. Of course. He was a man of action and he was acting on her information. Information gleaned from one of her nightmares.

Mala was finding the entire situation hard to process. She must have appeared stunned, for Aileen was still watching her, sympathy in her gaze.

Mala smiled up at her faintly. "Do I look that bad?"

"Like you've gone through the wringer." She turned on her heel. "I'm going to get you some food. And coffee."

Once she was gone, Mala rose on rather shaky legs and made her way into the bathroom. A shower helped clear her mind, but she wasn't going to relax until she heard back from Angus and learned of Sally's fate.

She'd never felt responsible for someone like this. Before the past week, her night terrors had been all about her and her whacked-out mind. But now? Now she was affecting other people's lives, possibly saving them, possibly failing to save them. Her mistakes might cost others dearly, and that responsibility was sudden and shocking.

Mala just prayed that John didn't get to Sally before Angus.

It took Angus eighteen hours to locate the she-wolf. In its way, the discovery was anticlimactic, thank God. Davies wasn't in the vicinity, and eventually, going from house to house— easier to accomplish in the dark with its shadows—he'd picked up the faint smell of a Sally covered by bleach and lemon.

She was still there. Some wolves might not have been able to scent her within that stink bomb, but he had. First, they'd secured the house. It was empty, as Mala had said. One of those new townhouses on sale and not yet bought. He'd gone in with Veronica, both of them human, along with two wolves to guard and protect them. Once they'd established there was no danger within, Veronica had called out Sally's name.

The first response was silence and stillness.

"We're here to help." Veronica rapped on the closed laundry-room door in the basement. "I'm coming in, okay?"

She'd signaled Angus to stay back as she opened the door. He couldn't see, but from the angle of Veronica's neck, she was looking down.

Then she crouched, keeping her body loose and non-threatening. "Hello, Sally."

Angus heard Sally let out a long, shaky breath.

"I'm Veronica. Werewolf, as you can tell. We learned you were in a bit of trouble."

"How do you know my name?" There was suspicion, but more than that, weariness, in the woman's question.

"We're a group of wolves concerned about John Davies's activities. We've been following him for a while." They'd decided talking about dream wraiths wasn't the best way to introduce themselves, whereas this explanation was suitably vague without veering away from the truth. He hoped it sounded reassuring to Sally.

"John Davies is trying to kill me," she said flatly, with little emotion. She could have been describing the weather.

"And that's why we're here. To prevent that." Veronica disappeared from Angus's sight as she approached Sally. "We want to take you somewhere safe. Have you heard of Wolf Town?"

The mumbled response was something not even Angus could make out, but the conversation continued between the two women. After a while, it was a matter of coaxing Sally out of the concrete, strong-smelling room that would one day be someone's laundry room. She wanted to know if Veronica was the only female here.

"Yes, I am," Veronica answered.

Sally wanted to know if Veronica lived in Wolf Town.

"No," Veronica admitted, but it didn't prevent her from convincing Sally to come with them. There were brief introductions to Angus and the other two wolves while Sally staying pasted to Veronica's side, after which they climbed into the minivan.

Angus put in a call to Jancis as they made their way to Veronica's house. By the time they arrived, Jancis was en route and would meet up with them before they headed back to Wolf Town together. Veronica herself had a family to stay with, not only a husband but children to raise. So Jancis would be Sally's reassurance instead of a car filled with unknown men.

In the meantime, Veronica and her older daughter kept Sally company. And everyone, drained by the past few days, slept.

Trey stayed away from the women. He was intimidating, didn't know how not to be, and while Angus played his laid-back, easygoing leader role as hard as possible, he kept to the background too.

All the while in the back of his mind, he continued to go over the fact that without Mala, they would never have found and saved this woman. Would never have known about her. Something critical had happened, something that could affect more wolves, and he needed to make sense of it in the larger scheme of things. He strongly felt that Mala had a role to play in the lives of those he cared about.

But before he could understand what Mala could accomplish, he had to get back home and bring Sally with him. Like a lot of weres, especially female, Sally had stayed in the shadows even after Wolf Town was founded. Not trusting humans, and not trusting other wolves.

She was late thirties, bedraggled, too thin and fragile. Veronica couldn't get more than vague background information out of her, though she didn't push for it either. It wasn't the time. Mostly they focused on making Sally comfortable before they traveled to Wolf Town, where she could learn to feel safe.

Not that they didn't need to take care of Davies, but first things first.

Trey pulled Angus aside and their focus slid away from Sally. Trey was shaking his head, a kind of disbelief still sitting on his face, no matter what this week had proved. "We learn something new every year, but this is incredible. I used to think finding a lynx shifter would be the biggest news in our world." His mouth quirked, acknowledging how personal that discovery was.

Angus had met the lynx, and Trey's husband, once. He had yet to meet a cougar shifter, though a handful were around southern Ontario. "I remember being shocked by the existence of cat shifters myself, and that was only ten years ago."

"And now we've got ourselves a dream wraith."

"I'd heard of the rumor or the myth, or whatever you want to call it, of dream wraiths."

Trey scratched his jaw. "In those stories they were always too powerful and too vulnerable. Perhaps that's why they seem to have disappeared."

Angus felt a shiver cross his back. "Are you saying they might have been killed off once they were identified?"

After a pause, Trey shrugged. "I doubt we can ever know what happened in the past. But you need to keep a guard on her, keep her protected. This is going to freak out some wolves. And this knowledge isn't going to stay between you, me and a small number of wolves, not with her contacting Sally and Caleb. Not with this recent dragnet we executed. Not with the way people in your town talk."

"I started this." He'd brought Mala out into the open.

"No," Trey said. "Don't give yourself too much credit. You and I both know who started it. Mala herself. She came searching for Wolf Town, for Caleb, for answers about her life. No doubt these are answers she needs to continue to function. Think about what it's been like for her."

The nightmares had probably been debilitating. Angus recognized that. Nevertheless, he didn't like what this all meant for Mala, and he was ready to jump in the car and drive back immediately, ensure she stay safe, make himself her personal guard, even if his new motto was supposed to be delegate, delegate, delegate.

But he couldn't leave until Jancis arrived. And Mala *was* being guarded. Among other things, he'd asked his beta to watch over her. He trusted Teo. "There's one thing I don't understand."

"Only one thing?" Trey drawled.

Angus ignored the comment. "Why wolves? It's not like humans aren't terrorized too. Why isn't she drawn to their fear in her dreams?"

"Do the blood test."

So Trey thought Mala might carry the wolf gene. "Jancis has no such dreams. Of that I'm certain."

"No, not everyone who's a carrier is going to be a wraith. But about fifteen years ago I ran into an old wolf who told old stories. And he talked about dream wraiths. I paid attention, even if I didn't believe, because some of our elders have knowledge that has been lost." Trey's mouth kicked up into that half-smile of his. "He had a theory about vampires too, which I'll tell you about sometime."

Angus felt his eyes widen. "They're not real."

"No. He figured they used to be."

"But he thought dream wraiths were related to wolves?"

"Yes, though he may not have meant by blood. The wraiths were a way of communicating back in the day when wolves had to be careful. But they were feared too. The power was mishandled, sometimes by the wraiths themselves, sometimes by those who controlled them."

"Mala only communicates with wolves who are being brutalized. At least, I believe that's how it goes."

"Mala also thought she was having nightmares. She hasn't been self-aware. She's been told her entire life that there's something wrong with her, has probably tried to find ways and means to end the dreams, avoid them. I doubt she's explored them or reached anything like her potential."

Angus didn't quite like Trey's tone, contemplative, but something extra too. As if Mala was a tool to be used.

"She's good," Angus declared. "Of that I'm certain." The first time he'd told Trey about his nose, years ago, he'd been less than impressed.

But times had changed and Trey dipped his head in acknowledgment. "Excellent. She can become a valuable part of our shifter community then."

As they heard a car drive up to the house, they both turned towards the front door. Jancis, Angus hoped. He didn't want to wait any longer. He needed to get home. On top of everything else, Caleb deserved a guardian who stayed around.

Trey touched his shoulder. "I'll come visit. Keep in touch, keep me informed."

Angus nodded and moved to the door, suddenly filled with pleasure at seeing his daughter on the front step.

"Thank you for coming." He stepped forward and hugged her. "How's Mala?"

She tilted her head, puzzled by his first question—and a little resentful. "Mala is fine. For some reason Aileen loves her, probably because you told her to and Aileen does anything you ask her to do."

Not anywhere near the truth, but Angus smiled and didn't respond to Jancis's resentful statement. Instead he asked, "How's Caleb?"

This question Jancis received with more approval, and Angus couldn't help but think Jancis didn't understand the scope of Mala's abilities. "Rory and Scott are taking good care of him."

Angus nodded. "As I thought."

"Where is she?" Jancis asked, done with pleasantries, the *she* referring to Sally.

"I'll introduce you, and then we need to leave."

The introductions were straightforward, with Sally looking wary, Jancis being interested but not effusive. Despite her at times abrupt manner, Jancis had a calm center that could draw people to her when she chose. As it happened, Sally was easily drawn. It was clear Sally wanted to find people whom she could trust. The weak smile, the worried eyes, even while she attempted to put on a game face, showed how vulnerable she felt.

A number of Angus's people had already headed home to Wolf Town, some with instructions to make sure Mala and Caleb stayed safe. So in the end four of them, including Jancis and Sally, piled into Jancis's car and started the long drive through the night, Angus at the wheel.

Veronica and Trey stood on the doorstep, Veronica waving, as they drove away.

130

Chapter Twelve

Mala stayed up until Angus called in with the news that they'd found Sally and she was safe, and Jancis was driving down to meet them. It was over, and Mala, with a bit of a pang, suggested that tomorrow it was time she go home.

Both Aileen and Eden looked alarmed, if not horrified, by the idea of it.

"Why?" Aileen asked, not a wail exactly, though if Aileen were the type to wail, it would have been.

"Honey," said Eden, who'd taken to calling her honey since she'd woken up from the second Sally dream yesterday. "You look terrible. You need to rest, not travel."

She wanted to sleep at home. But it was true, making that trip seemed close to impossible now, with her lack of energy. "I don't like sleeping," she muttered.

"You don't have to worry about Sally anymore," Aileen pointed out. "Angus is with her."

Eden nodded her agreement emphatically.

"Besides, Angus wants to see you again."

Yes, Angus and his wants. Very important around here. As it happened, Mala rather wanted to see Angus again. And Caleb. But first she'd like a little R and R from the B and B in Wolf Town, which had proved to be an incredibly draining experience, given her dreaming and her newfound realization of what her dreaming meant.

"I'd come back," Mala offered. But her words were weak. She couldn't face bussing over to North Bay and down to Toronto tomorrow. And no one was exactly chomping at the bit to offer her a drive home.

Eden frowned. "Do you have family in Toronto who are worried about you? Your mother?"

Mutely, Mala shook her head, unwilling to get into her relations with her family who all lived on the west coast anyway.

"Then you'll stay and we'll take care of you," Eden declared. "You're one of us now."

Mala realized she was gaping. The concept that she belonged somewhere, well, it made her laugh. Okay, she was getting punchy. So tired that she was in danger of becoming overly sentimental, maudlin even. Her chest seemed to swell with emotion.

Aileen swept Mala's bangs off her forehead, a soothing gesture. Wolves were very touchy-feely. Mala was surprised she didn't mind it.

"I'll stay next door," Aileen assured her, as if Mala was depending on her presence. "Knock on the wall if you need me."

"For goodness' sake, I don't need a keeper," Mala protested, gazing into the faces of two women, young and old, who both appeared utterly unconvinced by that statement. Which meant she must look a complete wreck.

Okay, sleep tonight, she told herself, *and figure out your place in the world tomorrow. Or at least figure out a way to get home.* The bigger issue of where she did and didn't belong might have to wait.

This active dreaming took such a chunk out of her, no question. Sometimes she thought she'd fade away with it.

But not this week. This week she had done some good and that fed something deep inside her. Gave her hope, though hope for what, she wasn't sure.

Short-term what she hoped for was dreamless dead-to-the-world sleep, sleep that would allow her energy to rise again. She'd need it if she ever wanted to leave Wolf Town.

As he approached home, Angus found his worst fear was that Mala would have bolted. Aileen had been left with instructions to do all she could to prevent such a leave-taking, and Angus had made it clear this was as much for Mala's sake as anyone else's. But Aileen had issues over any confinement, and her tone had said as much.

Angus's beta, Teo, was also keeping an eye on everyone, but if Aileen decided she was going to help Mala escape, it would be game over.

Angus rolled his eyes at himself. The rest of the occupants slept as he drove through the night, and early morning was threatening the dark now. Since when had he turned into such a worrier? Perhaps the day he'd taken on the project of Wolf Town. But Mala and her powers were bigger than anyone realized—that he felt in his gut. He reminded himself that she'd told him she would wait till he returned, and the promise would mean something to her.

He'd made the decision to assign Aileen to Mala because he believed Aileen would be the most likely person to persuade Mala to stay put, and he had to have some fucking trust in his own judgment.

Just like he'd been right to put Caleb into Rory and Scott's care.

It was an hour later when he pulled into his driveway, and Jancis blinked awake. He let his daughter rouse Sally and lead her into the house, while he went in to check on Caleb.

"He's fine, Dad." Rory emerged from the guest bedroom, fully alert despite having just woken up at their entry. "I think he missed you, even if Scott and I played a lot of three-handed Euchre, and Scott taught him World of Warcraft."

"World of Warcraft?" Angus groaned.

Rory grinned. "Don't be a dinosaur. I don't know why you have this thing against these games. It's not bad, he's interested and..." Rory lowered his voice to almost subvocal, "...it forces him to read."

"I suppose," Angus allowed grudgingly. And he did appreciate Scott's efforts though he had to be careful how he worded that appreciation, because Rory was quick to defend any perceived slight against his boyfriend. Even if Angus had gotten over Scott not being wolf months ago. So he nodded and said, "Thank Scott for me, if I don't get a chance to. But also? You two have to vacate that room. We're going to install Sally here."

"You bet." Rory didn't say it, but he'd be happy to return to the privacy of his own house.

"Okay, I need to give Eden a call and wake her up." But when Angus dialed through, she was up, preparing for the breakfast run at her restaurant.

"Mala is sleeping," Eden said, no preliminary greetings or welcome homes.

Relief swept over Angus. "Did she make any attempt to leave, do you know?"

"She talked about it in a halfhearted way, but the poor

thing's too worn out to travel. Besides, she lives alone, with no one waiting for her back in Toronto." Eden's tone signaled disapproval, not of Mala, but of Mala's family.

Angus figured this dreaming had isolated her. Well, that was one thing she had in common with shifters, feeling separate from the main population, having difficulties maintaining relationships with family and friends. With lovers.

"I don't think this dreaming stuff is good for her." The disapproval increased in Eden's voice, as if Angus were personally responsible for Mala's talent. Then again, he *had* asked Mala to search for Sally.

"I'm glad you're taking care of her, Eden. When she gets up, give me a shout, tell her I'm coming over to see her."

"All right." The dubious words were such a contrast to a few days ago where Mala was the interloper, not to be trusted. Now Angus was the one on the receiving end of Eden's mistrust. He didn't bother to defend himself. For one thing, he wanted Eden to feel protective of Mala. For another, he couldn't regret having found Sally.

So he hung up and refocused on home. A call came in from Trey who wanted a brief update, and then Caleb was up and awake, trying not to look excited by the fact Angus had returned.

When Angus gave the boy a hug, Caleb hugged back hard, clinging for a brief moment, and Angus smiled. "It's good to see you."

At that point, Caleb's expression turned bashful so they focused on food and eating, while Sally was introduced to everyone, including Caleb. No one bothered to point out they'd both been terrorized by Davies, though Caleb, at least, knew as much.

Eventually Caleb went off to school, rather reluctantly, so

Angus accompanied him on the walk over. Then Sally went to sleep in the guestroom, Rory and Scott left for their house, and Jancis and Angus did some work from home.

"Work" was becoming something of a misnomer, given that of late Angus did little of it. Though that would change in the next month or so, when renovation contracts picked up.

By noon, Eden still hadn't called and Angus decided that instead of eating at home, he'd lunch at Eden's and find out what was what with Mala. Perhaps see Aileen.

As he walked into Eden's, she announced, "Mala's not up yet."

"Yes, thanks, Eden, I figured as much."

"Aileen needs a break."

Angus lifted his eyebrows. With all that had been going on, he hadn't given careful thought to Aileen's unusual needs. She'd been human for all of...five days? He rubbed his forehead. Time was all running together, with nights spent driving or running as wolf.

"Where is she?"

"Upstairs, in the room to the right of Mala's. Aileen told Mala she'd stay and watch over her while she slept. I've kept Aileen fed, but she's pacing the floor like a caged animal."

"Give me my meal and I'll take it up, boot her out of there."

Eden gave a curt nod, and not too long after, Angus was walking up the stairs, tray in hand. He knocked and Aileen answered, looking a little wild-eyed, her body vibrating with unused energy. *Time to go, honey*, Angus thought.

Without preamble, Aileen declared somewhat desperately, "I told Mala I'd wait here until she woke up."

"I'll take your place, keep your word for you."

Aileen paused, her body tightening, caught between her

promise to Mala and the lure of freedom. Sometimes she took things too literally, and sometimes not literally enough.

"Mala is counting on you in particular being here when she wakes up?" Angus asked.

Aileen frowned. "I don't know. She said she didn't need a keeper, but she liked the idea of me waiting. When I assured her I would be, I smelled relief."

"Okay. But Mala is comfortable with me. She'll be okay with the switch, don't you think?"

Aileen pulled in a breath and gave a sharp nod. "I think so. I'd stay anyway, I don't like to break my word but I..." Her shoulders sagged in defeat. She usually didn't give a damn that she didn't function well as human, but for once it mattered to her. This was progress.

He placed a hand on her shoulder. "Hey, you did good."

She slid her gaze up to his. "I could have done worse."

"Everything takes time."

"Right. In three decades I'll be normal. Maybe."

"None of us are normal, Aileen. Not even Mala." He tipped his head towards the door. "Now, get out of here."

Aileen didn't bother with her jacket but sped out of the room and down the stairs. Whatever chill she picked up would soon be dispelled by the heat of her shift.

Once she was gone, Angus sat down and listened. The walls weren't thin, but his hearing was enough that he'd pick up noise if Mala was moving about. He heard nothing.

He wondered how long she would sleep. Then he wondered how healthy this dreaming was for her. It was noon, and if she hadn't woken by four p.m., he'd enter the room—after a brief knock—and make certain she was okay. It was a fine balance between respecting her privacy and ensuring that she hadn't sickened from these wraith visits, the last of which had been demanded by him.

Less than two hours later, Mala stirred. No footsteps, but Angus was glad she had a bed that creaked, however softly. When nothing more came of it, he decided it was time. He left his laptop in Aileen's room and walked the very short way down the hall to Mala's door.

At his rap, the bed creaked again, and she cleared her voice before she got out an "I'm awake, Aileen," her tone welcoming.

He liked the trust in her voice. Aileen had done better than she knew. Turning the knob, he warned, "It's me." He stepped into the room.

She sat, eyes widening as if he were an alien of some sort, and the wan expression on her face spoke volumes. "Where's Aileen?"

"She had to go," he said dryly. How to explain Aileen's drives and needs to a non-wolf? "It's too easy for Aileen to feel claustrophobic when she spends time inside."

Mala frowned.

"How are you feeling?"

She blinked a few times, trying to make herself more awake for this conversation, he guessed. "I've been better."

"You heard we found her, the woman in your dreams? I want to thank you for that. A lot of us want to thank you for what you've accomplished this week."

Mala nodded, her expression lightening as if pleased. "How is Sally?"

Angus shrugged. "Physically not too bad. I can't tell about the rest of it. She's had a rough time."

Looking away, Mala moved to the side of the bed. He could tell she wanted him to leave, but she wore flannel pajamas, so he didn't think modesty was a huge concern. She scrubbed her face and spoke straight ahead. "I'll be down soon."

He didn't like the way her body seemed so fragile, a slight tremor there. "Can you stand?"

She jerked her gaze to him, her expression turning indignant. "Of course I can." To prove it, she pushed to her feet and stumbled. He was beside her immediately, taking an arm to steady her.

"Is it always like this?" he asked in a low voice. "After the real-world dreaming?"

For a moment, she stayed stiff in his grasp, before she slumped against him. He brought an arm around her shoulders, ready to catch her.

"I'm not going to fall this time." She turned her face towards him, muffling her voice. "I'm just so tired afterwards. I usually take a week off work from exhaustion following a nightmare. And then I get fired."

"No one's firing you here." It was odd, her leaning against him and yet she wouldn't actually embrace him. He pushed hair off her face. "Mala? I'm worried you're going to collapse."

"No." She stepped away, stronger now. "I can navigate the bathroom all on my own, I promise. But maybe you can bring me up a sandwich or something. Whatever Eden has."

"You bet." He watched her enter the small bathroom attached to the room. She expected him to leave right away, but he waited a few minutes, fearing she might faint in there. When she didn't, he exited the room to fetch some food for her. He also phoned the town's doctor.

Chapter Thirteen

That the emotion she felt most keenly was embarrassment annoyed Mala. It was because of the dreaming. She needed to be alone, when her nerves were so easily frayed, not staying with strangers. She understood what she'd done was significant and life changing for herself and others—to actively search out someone in her dreams. But to process it in Wolf Town, well, it was something she shied away from.

Go through the motions now and figure out what it means later, she told herself.

Normally she spent a week on her own recovering, going easy on herself, sleeping and eating and watching TV. This was proving more difficult to accomplish in Eden's B and B, especially with Angus popping in to wake her up. She'd almost fallen down in front of him again, when twice in a lifetime was more than enough.

She shook her head. *Don't focus on the embarrassment.* Which was easier said than done outside the solitude of her Toronto apartment. Here she had to talk to people, including Angus, and that was both wonderful and awful. He unsettled her and settled her at the same time, and she didn't know how that was even possible.

Upon waking, she'd expected Aileen to be around and had been shocked to have Angus walk into her room. Yet when he'd taken her arm, a kind of relief had flowed through her, as if she'd been waiting for him to do just that. She hoped he hadn't minded her leaning against him. He didn't seem to.

She splashed her face and took her time in the bathroom, partly because she wasn't at her most coordinated, being sleep-groggy and wiped out, and partly because she hoped Angus would be gone by the time she exited the washroom.

The room was empty, but five minutes later he returned with a smorgasbord, and Eden in tow. Eden marched over to put a hand on Mala's forehead like she had a fever.

"I'm not sick," Mala protested.

"You need to eat."

"I will." At Mala's assurance, Eden simply glared at Angus, as though everything in the world was his fault. Mala could have sworn that when Angus was away, Eden had attributed everything good in the world to him. Perhaps that's what came of being all-powerful in this small community.

"You need to figure out a few things." Eden wagged her finger at the alpha and sailed out of the room before Mala understood what she meant by that admonishment.

"I always do," Angus half-murmured, though Eden wouldn't hear him. Then he was placing the tray in front of Mala. To her relief, she was hungry. Sometimes after the dreams, the nausea induced by what she'd witnessed made it hard to eat, and not eating slowed her recovery.

But today the dream wolf was safe—and Sally was not even a dream. That knowledge churned her stomach, but not enough to kill her appetite.

Before Mala was a quarter done with her food, a knock came at the door. She looked to Angus who appeared unsurprised.

"Keep eating. I'll be back." He moved out of the room, leaving the door ajar. She heard soft, deep voices.

Mentally she shrugged, figuring Angus had all kinds of important things to do and people to see. At least someone didn't want to see her. However, the minute she finished eating, laying down her fork, Angus poked his head back in. Which had her wondering how good his hearing was. Alarmingly good?

"Mala? I'd like to introduce you to someone."

She frowned. She was in her pajamas and felt like crap. Did he have to insist on this? Hadn't she met enough denizens of Wolf Town?

He took her non-answer for compliance and a man followed Angus in. His expression, a sympathetic quirk of his lips implying he understood how she felt about the situation, disarmed her. She hoped he would soon leave. But instead, Angus said, "Teo, this is Mala, the woman who has helped save two of our own."

Our own. Mala imagined what it would be like to be referred to as that after a matter of days. So welcoming on such short notice. Well, *she* wasn't a wolf, was she? God knows what she was. She didn't, and neither did anyone else.

"And Mala..." Angus kept his eyes on hers, clearly trying to read her expression, "...this is Teo, Wolf Town's doctor."

No. Her body stiffened up at the thought of seeing a doctor. Angus had *no right*. She forced herself to keep her words steady, reasonable, to *not* get overemotional and easy to dismiss. "I don't need a doctor, thank you very much."

To his credit, Angus didn't slide his gaze over to Teo but remained focused on her. "You've done a lot for us, Mala, and we want to make sure you're all right."

"I am all right," she said.

"I want to take your blood pressure and pulse," Teo put in calmly. Like Angus, he had a nice voice, though it sounded more professional than friendly the way Angus's did. He didn't crowd her but waited for her permission.

"I'm fine," she insisted.

"Mala." The pleading note in Angus's voice surprised her. "I asked you for a huge favor when you went looking for Sally. I want to make sure it did you no harm."

"It didn't. I promise you. I always feel exhausted after dreaming, that's all." This reaction of hers was familiar, for better and worse, but Angus didn't look convinced.

"Not a full physical," Teo assured her. "Just a cuff around your upper arm."

She could keep arguing, she could sit and say nothing, but both men seemed so...sincere. Plus, and this was key, they were waiting for her assent. She sighed.

"All right," she said rather gracelessly. Her tendency to wear overlarge pajamas meant loose sleeves, and she rolled one up so he could fit the black armband around her. Next she submitted to his careful fingers on her wrist as he counted her pulse, then his stethoscope on her chest and back, and finally his request that he check her throat for some infection or another. At least he didn't insist he take her temperature.

By the end she was rather cross but not sullen enough to point out this had been more than a cuff around her arm. Admittedly she felt a lot less shaky than when she'd first woken up.

It occurred to her that it might be healthier to be distracted by people after her dream rather than caught up in her own thoughts that became a nightmarish merry-go-round, circling back to the terror she'd just emerged from. Well, it hadn't been a terror, it was true, but Sally had felt so alone, so despairing, and those feelings lingered within.

"Mala?"

She focused. She supposed she'd been drifting, because the twin concern on the two men's faces was a little oppressive. She tried on a smile.

Teo's dark eyes held her gaze as he delivered his verdict. "Everything's within the normal range, though your blood pressure is on the high side and I'd like to check that again. Do you know what's normal for you?"

"Usually it's low," she admitted. "I don't remember exactly but less than the standard 120 over 80."

"You're 130 over 92. I'll take your blood pressure in a couple of days and compare, but I wouldn't be surprised to learn this dreaming ability of yours is a stressor."

She tried not to snort out loud in laughter.

Teo smiled, and his rather stolid if sympathetic expression transformed into something very attractive, approachable. "You wouldn't be surprised either, right?"

"No," she muttered. "I sometimes get headaches."

"Ah."

She liked him. She liked Angus, but she needed to set them straight, given that Teo believed she'd be here two days from now for more doctor visits. "I can't stay any longer. I have to return home and look for a job."

There, that sounded reasonable. She hadn't made it sound like she was anxious to retreat into her hidey-hole.

Still she added, "My money's running out, you see."

For the first time, the men did look at each other, not so much to talk over her, she felt, but to avoid her gaze. Then Angus stared directly at her, apology in his face.

"That's not a good idea, Mala."

She cleared her throat. "It's not up to you though, is it?"

Teo lifted one eyebrow in a way that suggested Angus needed to deal with this, not him. "If you'll excuse me." He nodded at Mala. "It was very nice to meet you, and I appreciate what you've done for us. You've gone above and beyond."

She opened her mouth to protest, but he slipped out of the room before she could say anything.

"I'll offer you a job," Angus said abruptly.

She looked at him in disbelief. "You don't know my work. How can you offer me a job?"

His blue eyes gleamed. "Very easily. There's work to be had here."

She rose from her bed, because she didn't like him gazing down at her from quite such a great height.

"You belong with us, Mala."

Hadn't she been envious of Caleb and Sally being welcomed so wholeheartedly? And he was offering the same thing to her. But she wasn't a wolf and never would be. She didn't trust the offer. She'd been in families before where it became clear she didn't belong. "Do I?"

He nodded. "I don't understand what you can do, what you can achieve, but it's clear you have a connection to wolves."

"Achieve?"

He was talking in a way that she found incredibly odd—as if she was useful. When her dreams had always been debilitating, always took away and offered her nothing in return.

Angus reached out an arm and drew her to him. She didn't resist. She found it impossible to resist. But she couldn't relax either, and he must have found it strange, holding her as she stood stiffly within his arms.

145

"Mala," he whispered across her ear. He said her name a lot and for some reason she loved to hear it. Yet she found herself shaking her head. "I want to protect you."

Her laugh was muffled by him, by his broad chest, and she felt herself snuggling in there. That same relief as earlier flowed through her. She'd been an affectionate child, her mother had always told her that, but during the estrangement with her parents she'd withdrawn from shows of physical affection, and since then she sometimes craved it.

That's what was going on here. Angus was a physical guy. The thing that puzzled her was the fact she'd developed an aversion to touch over the years. Where had that gone?

He was rubbing a circle on her back and she had to stop herself from sighing in reaction. Was this some type of werewolf magic?

His words filtered back to her: *I want to protect you.*

She picked up the thread of that conversation. "Who or what do you want to protect me against?"

His chest rose and fell against her as he took in a breath and delivered the answer: "Caleb's father."

"But he only caught my first name." There were plenty of Malas, at least in the city. "In the dream," she added, in case that wasn't clear.

The hazy contented feeling of being held vanished as Angus's hands clamped down on her arms, and he jerked her away so he could look into her eyes, his alarm clear.

"What?" His face had turned stone cold and she didn't like it. She wanted to retreat, but he didn't release her. "He caught your name? How?"

"Please let go of me."

He did so, though not her gaze, and she couldn't bring

herself to look away. "Mala, please tell me how Davies knows your name."

She rubbed a hand across her eyes to break their eye contact. "He heard me, I mean he felt me inside him, a presence, and when I heard you saying my name, he heard it too. It's too easy to communicate when I'm inside someone. It's as if our thoughts are shared." She glanced at him, wondering what he made of that oddness. "I didn't mean for John Davies to get that information..."

His expression loosened from that severe flat look to one of guilt.

"Jesus Christ." He closed his eyes and pivoted away from her. Then he turned back, touched her forehead so lightly with his blunt, square finger that she shivered. "Mala."

There was a kind of despair when he said her name and she didn't understand it.

"I've put you in danger. Do you understand? This town talks among each other. I do not rule with an iron fist or any such thing. Everyone knows about you. It will not be hard for Davies to send someone here to find you. And if you go back home, it will not be hard for him to find you there."

She stared back at him, dumbfounded. She couldn't believe this made sense. Because, despite the proof of what she could do, the dreams still seemed to be something that was all in her head. Her dreams had always been her own stupid problem.

"You need to stay with me," said Angus grimly.

She shouldn't like the sound of that so much. Besides... "He can find me more easily here than in Toronto."

"True," Angus agreed. "But here, Davies would have to go through me and the rest of the town first."

Chapter Fourteen

Angus took over Eden's B and B, small as it was. One room for Aileen, one for himself, and Mala's sandwiched between them. He would have preferred that Mala move into his house, but with Jancis, Caleb and Sally there, it was too crowded.

He needed a bigger house, but that was a project for later.

He'd persuaded Mala to remain in Wolf Town for a temporary stay. It wasn't, perhaps, his finest hour, working on her fear like that. But he wasn't making up stories. Davies was dangerous and, with Angus's help, knew Mala's name and had some idea of what she could accomplish.

Angus now had three people under his protection who were threatened by Caleb's father. While Angus didn't relish taking another life, he was preparing himself to do just that. There was no other recourse when it came to sociopathic werewolves, and Davies had proved himself to be one.

Caleb cleared his throat, and Angus left his thoughts alone to focus on the boy who was lingering in the threshold of the kitchen. It bothered Angus that Caleb felt he needed permission to enter the kitchen when Angus was in it, and it made Angus wonder how welcoming some of his mother's friends and acquaintances had been.

"Looking for something to eat?" Angus asked. "We'll be disappointed if you're not eating as much as you want whenever you want. It's considered bad form in Wolf Town."

Caleb's slight frown indicated he didn't quite know how to respond, but he dug into the fridge, which was the main thing. Meanwhile Angus finished making the coffee.

As Caleb chomped down on his hastily made sandwich, he asked, "Are you going away again soon?"

Angus poured his coffee. "I'm staying here, where I have people to look after, including you."

"I don't need to be looked after."

Jancis strolled into the kitchen. "Doesn't matter, Caleb. That's Dad's only way to function, to look after people. He doesn't know how to exist otherwise."

"Thanks, Jancis. I think," Angus said dryly, though she had saved the conversation. Caleb didn't need to be told things quite so baldly as Angus just had. His ward was teen boy enough to need his independence.

"If it wasn't for my dad, I'd be fine," Caleb insisted.

"And so would Sally," said Jancis. "But you're not fine because he's not letting it be fine. So we'll all deal with it. You don't have to take this personally, you know. It's clear he'd be after someone, if it wasn't you, and he needs to be stopped."

"Mala stopped him," Caleb said.

"Yes, and we're glad for it. Very glad." Angus set his cup on the counter, careful not to let anger get the better of him. "But it's not something we can count on."

Caleb met his gaze, brown eyes dark and deep. "I want to kill him."

That reaction didn't surprise Angus, but he would not put such a burden on Caleb's young shoulders. No one should have to kill their father. And no one under Angus's watch was going to.

Once the house was quieter, Caleb at school and Jancis at work, Sally made her way into the kitchen. She was a slight woman, if tall, small-boned and too thin. Not surprising for a werewolf on the run. But she compared poorly to someone like Aileen who was wiry and strong. Angus hoped that Sally could regain some of her health here.

His mind went to Mala, briefly. She was soft in a way werewolves weren't. She curled into him on occasion, more physically affectionate than he might have expected a human to be.

"I don't think I properly thanked you." The words were quiet but terse, as if Sally expected a price to be paid for having been rescued and put in a safe place.

"We were all glad to help." He made it a point that it was not about him. Huge favors owed to alphas had something of a historical basis, and they didn't always bode well for the one who did the owing.

She eyed him—that mix of wariness and anger he was not unfamiliar with. They were of an age, and female werewolves were coveted by males. She could still bear children.

But none of it meant anything to him, to his libido, to his dreams of family. For one thing, he had family. Something that would be useful for him to emphasize. "You've met my daughter, Jancis, of course."

Sally was taken aback, searching for his hidden meaning and deciding he wanted gratitude. "Yes. She's been very kind."

Angus allowed himself a crooked smile. "She's not always kind. She has to like someone first."

Sally fiddled with the spoon she'd picked up as she stood by the counter, not yet comfortable enough to sit down. "She's...old to be your daughter. And doesn't look much like you."

"I'm an adoptive parent. Jancis's twin, Rory, is also mine. Caleb's my ward. I've had other wards over the years." He wasn't going to say he was done with parenting, because he wasn't. But he could see something in Sally's tense body relax.

With that he rose, because he suspected Sally would be able to eat more when he wasn't around. "Jancis will be back at lunch, for her break. I'm heading over to the local B and B. I'll return around the time Caleb's done with school, and I'll probably see you then."

Sally nodded, her dirty-blonde hair falling in her eyes.

"You're safe here, Sally," he assured her. "No one is going to force you to do anything you don't want to do."

Mala sat at the counter, munching on her early lunch and finding herself amused by the contrast between today and last week when she'd first walked in here. For one thing, Eden hadn't kidnapped her credit card. In fact, Eden refused to touch her credit card, all things being charged to Angus.

Which was plain weird. She felt a bit like a kept woman. Well, apart from the fact that Angus didn't regard her in that light. Fortunately no one was around to see her face heating at her own thoughts. She tried very hard to put the crush away, once and for all. She'd take it out again when she'd returned home and was no longer at risk of running into the alpha.

That's what half the town called him.

On cue, the door flew open, caught by the wind, and in stomped Angus, brushing the snow off his jacket. At least he no longer thought she was a threat to Caleb. As she lifted her gaze to meet his, a smile greeted her, warmth in those eyes.

She'd seen this expression of his when Caleb or his kids entered the room, when almost anyone entered the room. Part of being the alpha appeared to involve being genuinely happy to greet and talk to everyone. It must be an interesting way to live. The awful thought that she was going to miss Wolf Town when she left crossed her mind, and she pushed it away. Just as she pushed away the crush.

Who walked right up to her. For God's sake she was too old for this.

"Hi there, Mala. How are you feeling this morning?"

Shy. "Good." She didn't want to appear tongue-tied so she added, "I slept well."

"I'm glad to hear it."

"No dreams, of the regular or irregular kind." She was trying to forestall the questions by answering them preemptively. It made the conversation feel more normal, less like therapy, or like she was a strange creature he needed to better comprehend.

Something of her thoughts must have shown, because the warmth receded, replaced by a look that suggested he was searching for the real meaning behind her words.

Then he quirked a smile at her. "I wasn't asking for a report, Mala, though I'm glad to hear all this."

"It's weird talking about it," she confessed. "I've spent years *not* talking about it, avoiding it or being shut down if I tried to say anything about my dreams. So..." She shrugged. "It's a little freeing, in its way."

He nodded.

"Part of me is relieved that I know it's real, because it always felt so real," she continued, unable to stop, though they were in public and he'd only asked how she was. "But part of me is appalled at what I've witnessed over the course of my life."

He dropped a hand on her shoulder, a warm, broad hand, and she wanted to lean into him. He probably wouldn't even mind, and she couldn't decide if that was good or bad. As if he read her thoughts, he slid that palm down her back, a caress, and she breathed in deeply.

He retreated. This was normal for wolves, she reminded herself. She'd read a lot about them during that week-long study session before she took the bus north. Though she couldn't say for sure that Canadian newspapers provided expert content on the subject. But wolves were physically affectionate. If nothing else, this might indicate that Angus liked her as a person.

Or a tool, a tiny voice said. It had become increasingly clear that the wolves in Wolf Town regarded her as having a special ability that meant she belonged to them, and she didn't know what to think about that. While it was nice to belong somewhere, to be acknowledged as a wraith—another new word she'd learned—took her aback. How much did they care about who the wraith actually was?

Maybe it didn't matter.

"It's a burden," Angus stated, and Mala had to go back to her last words, about being appalled at what she'd witnessed in her dreams for so many years. "Power often is to those who care about its effects on others."

She glanced up at him to see fellow-feeling there. Well, they had that to share, though her alarming, erratic dreams didn't quite compare to someone who took responsibility for an entire town of wolves and their brethren.

What was she thinking, that they had so much in common? She barely knew the man and her emotions were beginning to alarm her.

"What happens next?" She expected more charm, more warmth, he had such a supply of it and she had little protection against it, but instead he studied the menu on the chalkboard.

"I am trying to convince you to stay with us," he said, his voice low, his gaze turned forward as he settled on the stool beside her. "Tell me about your life in Toronto."

She blew out a breath. "There's not much to tell."

"Family?"

"They're in BC. We're not close. My father got fed up with my foibles. I decided to travel east and start a new life." Which had ended up feeling like the old life in a different place.

"They cut you loose."

"It was painful for all involved. My parents are used to having a lot of family around. But my two brothers can fill the gap." She paused. "What about your family?"

"You've met my children."

"Yes. I was wondering about your parents."

"Dead."

"I'm sorry."

He grimaced and his tone was flat. "Don't be. I'm not."

Her eyes widened. Yes, she had issues with her parents but never would she wish them dead.

He didn't smile when he turned to her. "I don't mean to shock you. But Davies is not the only werewolf who has turned violent like this."

"Oh." Then, staring at his eyes which were a brilliant blue, she remembered. "One of the monsters..."

He cocked his head, an encouraging gesture.

"...he, the wolf in my older dreams, he appeared a number of times." She gave a sharp shake of her head. For God's sake she was capable of speaking clearly. She pulled in a breath to try again. "In my teens, I'd have what I considered a recurring nightmare, with variations. The wolf tended to be the same. He had your color of eye." Though the eyes themselves were so different: ice versus warmth, harsh versus caring, monster versus Angus.

He frowned. "How old are you?"

"Twenty-eight."

"So it ended eight years ago?"

"Yes."

"That would coincide with Gabriel's death." Angus pointed to the corner of one of his eyes. "We had a similar eye color, yes. No doubt distantly related, though it's difficult to track parentage among us. Children get abandoned. Fathers don't stay around. The gene is passed through the mother."

"They look different on you," she said softly, because though his manner was amiable it also seemed a little forced, as if she might have hurt him in some way.

At that, he sent her a wry smile. "I would hope so."

She pushed the rest of her food around her plate for something to do. "After that wolf disappeared from my dreams, died, I guess..." It was odd thinking of the monster that way. Back then, after he'd finally left her alone, she'd thought her mind had become stronger and was no longer indulging in the bloody terrors of the blue-eyed one. "Well, I had a break for two years. I thought the dreams were over for me."

"How many times have you dreamed of Davies?"

"The dreams with Caleb and Sally, that's it."

"That might mean his behavior is deteriorating," Angus said grimly. "That before he was holding himself back in some way." His voice became even lower. "He has to be stopped."

She put her hands to her cheeks and shook her head, fending off the feeling of being overwhelmed. "It is so strange talking to you like this, as though my observations matter. It's

155

so matter of fact. So—"

"—*real*," he finished. "You'll let me protect you until we figure this out, won't you?"

She wasn't going to make a rash promise again, like when she'd told him she would stay and a day turned into more than a week. "I can't know that. I can't know anything about how this will play out."

He accepted that with a nod and changed the topic. "It's time you came to my place and met Sally. In flesh and blood."

"I want to meet her. Is that strange? That I want to meet the people I see in my dreams?" It had happened before, this longing, but she'd never been able to take it seriously, only as an indicator of her unhealthy loneliness.

"I don't think so," he said, rising.

As he guided her out the door, she didn't feel lonely, when that had been such a constant companion. She hugged her crush close, hiding it, as she walked beside him, into the early spring's wind and snow, and they made their way to his house.

Chapter Fifteen

Sally looked different in person, of course she did. It wasn't a dream, and Mala wasn't inside someone else. She wondered if something of the same thought had gone through Sally's mind after Angus's brief introduction where he touched glancingly on the point that Mala had helped them find Sally.

She was regarding Mala with deep suspicion.

"Would you like a coffee?" Angus asked Mala, who said yes in order to have something in her hands. He left the living room, and that meant she and Sally were facing each other.

Sally made a point of looking away.

It wasn't that Mala expected gratitude, the entire situation was too weird for that, but clearly Sally didn't consider that they had any connection she was interested in.

Mala bit down on her lip. Caleb had seemed keen to recognize Mala and understand what had happened between them. But there was no reason to believe everyone would react the same way.

When Angus returned, Sally gazed up at him deferentially, as if awaiting his command, while Angus's easy expression appeared to stiffen.

She was glad Angus didn't like deferential. In fact, Mala guessed he was uncomfortable with it. He passed Mala a cup of coffee and sat on the couch beside her with his. Sally hadn't wanted a drink.

Angus leaned forward to look at the woman across from them. "Sally, we need to know how you met John Davies."

Sally's gaze cut to Mala, her way of saying she didn't want Mala there, and Angus didn't acknowledge it.

"I didn't," she bit out, eyes downcast and at odds with her angry tone. "He found me, chased me, demanded that I come with him. I escaped. He chased me some more." She paused and her lip curled. "Some wolves are like that, you know."

"I know," said Angus.

Sally indicated Mala. "She's not a wolf. Why is she here?"

Angus scratched his jaw. "Jancis isn't a wolf either. That's not how we decide who is in and who is out."

Sally persisted. "Your daughter is related to a wolf."

"And Mala has a connection to wolves," Angus remarked.

Sally shrugged, her body language screaming that she didn't want to talk or even be with them.

At that point, Caleb slammed inside the house, Rory close behind, shaking off the heavy, wet March snow that continued to fall. Caleb's face lit up at the sight of Angus and when he turned to Mala, he kept his smile. "Hi, Mala."

"Hey, Caleb. How are you doing?"

"All right." Then he added, since that didn't seem to be enough of an answer, "School was okay."

She recalled her brothers and how they weren't great on specifics. "Good."

Caleb was taking in the three of them, and with a glance back at Rory he said, too loudly, "So, do we have a plan?"

Mala could fill in the gaps, a plan to handle Caleb's father.

She hated that Davies had done this to his own son.

Angus shook his head. "Not yet. We're working on it."

"As far as we can tell, he's gone to ground." Angus met Teo's solemn gaze.

Teo's disgruntled expression deepened. "Have you told them?"

"Caleb, Sally and Mala know, if that's who you're asking about."

"Who's got them?"

"Rory's watching Caleb, except at school when Harrison has him. Aileen and I keep an eye on Sally and Mala, switching off, and sometimes I call in backup."

"Do Sally and Mala know they have bodyguards?"

Angus nodded. He wasn't much for secrets. Secrets had done werewolves too much harm in general.

"You and Aileen will be kept too busy."

With a sigh, Angus acknowledged Teo's point. "I introduced them yesterday, Mala and Sally. It didn't go over well. They were both nervous, but Sally was freaked out. I could barely refer to the fact that Mala's a dream wraith."

"Well not everyone is going to be pleased with having had a wraith present in their body," Teo said slowly. "If I'm understanding the experience."

"That presence saved Sally's life." Angus knew he sounded defensive and insensitive about Sally's trauma. But he couldn't help it when it came to Mala.

Teo's brief smile said as much. "I'm not arguing that. We're talking about Sally's discomfort not Mala's motivation."

"Jancis is good with Sally. She seems to relax with her." It bothered Angus though. He wanted to build an environment here so Mala could feel at home, but Sally's anxiety wasn't the best first step. It was hard to blame the poor woman, but in the grand scheme of things Angus worried her reaction to Mala would be the common one.

"So. What do you need from me?" Teo asked. This was their weekly meeting, part of Angus's program to delegate and not take everything on his shoulders. He supposed for such a strategy to be effective he needed to broaden the members of the meeting beyond two, and hold it in a more communal space than Teo's living room.

Later. Now Angus had a specific request. "I want you to test Mala, see if she has the wolf gene."

Teo's eyebrows rose in surprise and disapproval. Testing was frowned upon, the blood test feared. It had the potential to be used for a witch hunt if the mainstream populace ever turned on shifters. Or, if a small group of powerful people got their hands on the information, they could attempt to utilize shifters for their own ends.

Neither scenario was all that far-fetched, despite how calmly they lived now in Wolf Town.

Davies, for example, could fuck up the peace that existed between shifters and the regular population.

"He has to be eliminated." Angus let the anger show in his voice.

Teo frowned.

Crap, Angus was thinking too much and not talking enough. Old habit. He leaned forward, elbows on knees, and focused on his beta. "Sorry. I want you to test Mala off the record. I want to find out if she has a biological connection to us. As to who has to be eliminated..." Angus closed his eyes. He disliked killing, though he had a number of executions under his belt, nothing he'd ever tell humans about.

"John Davies." Teo supplied the name.

Angus echoed it. "Davies."

"Who has gone to ground. Is Trey trying to track him down?"

"Yep."

"Close to impossible if he's turned wolf and is staying wolf." Teo's expression turned contemplative. "Unless Mala can work her magic."

Angus pulled a face. "It harms her, and that will require that Davies is actively terrorizing someone."

"It's something to explore."

"No doubt."

Teo's face went still, suspicious. "You like her."

"Sure I like her."

Teo didn't blink. That was something Angus appreciated in Teo, his straight talking and his ability to zero in on what was important. He only wished it didn't involve this—Angus's growing feelings for Mala.

"It's nothing very deep." Angus found he didn't like this halfhearted denial. "No, that's not what I mean. It might be deep, but it is new. We've been thrown together. She's vulnerable, because of the way things have played out, and I don't like to be asking her to give so much of herself. I don't know what we're giving back to her. It runs too close to the line of using someone."

Teo reached for his coffee finally. He always drank it cold. "Aileen says Mala is her friend."

"I'm glad to hear it."

"Aileen doesn't declare people her friends often, you know that. But more, that means Aileen won't allow Mala to be used by us if she can help it. Nor will you." Teo yawned. "I'm exhausted. Long day at the clinic. I'll get on that blood test and keep the results quiet. You and I and Mala can talk about it afterwards. Once I've informed Mala either way, that is, and I have her permission to talk to you."

Teo believed in doctor-patient confidentiality.

"Of course."

"Meanwhile, we're in a holding pattern." Teo waited for Angus to confirm that last statement. Then he paused and Angus found he was bracing himself for a doctor-like statement. "I hope, Angus, you're not taking some kind of weird responsibility for Davies's violence."

"Nope."

"Davies is responsible for the actions of Davies," Teo intoned, then grinned at Angus's evident irritation.

"As I've told Caleb." As someone once told Angus about his own father.

"All right." Teo grinned again, this time a slyer expression. "Better go check on Mala on your way home tonight."

Angus rose. "Good night, Teo."

"If you and Aileen are offering Mala true friendship, I think that's worth quite a lot to someone who has few family and friends to depend upon."

Friendship. It really wasn't how Angus thought of Mala, but that didn't mean it wasn't true. He inclined his head to acknowledge Teo's point. Teo stood and they shook hands before Angus clapped him on the back. Then Angus left. He hadn't told Teo, but he wasn't going home tonight. Aileen and Jancis were holding down the fort while Angus stayed at the B and B to watch over Mala.

Rory, Angus's son, was a very pleasant young man. Okay, he wasn't *that* much younger than her, a year or two maybe. But Mala rather wished she had a way of telling him he could leave now.

Instead he poured himself another coffee.

"Actually," he said, "I can't leave. Not until Dad arrives."

She sometimes wondered if these people could read her mind.

He laughed. "Don't look so alarmed. Your face is easy to read, which isn't a bad thing," he added quickly. "And..." He came to realize he wasn't making the situation better.

"Is this something you can smell?" she asked in disbelief.

"Uh, well, sorta." He cast around for a better spin. "Because of our senses we can read people quite well, but *not* their minds."

"But your boyfriend..." Mala's question trailed off. Scott was a Minder, Angus had casually dropped that bomb one time, and before she could ask more on the subject, his phone had rung, ending the conversation.

Rory's pleasant expression changed to one of defensiveness. "*No.* Scott doesn't read minds. And while he can make people think or do things they wouldn't have done, he doesn't. Especially not here where wolves are unaffected by his ability. That's why he likes Wolf Town."

"Well, he's a bit like me then. Not that I'm living here," she added hastily, "but we are both among wolves and have...different abilities." She didn't know how to describe what she could do. People called her a wraith, but it had a cold, spectral ring to it that she didn't find endearing or even positive.

Rory cocked his head and smiled, warm again, and she saw how like his father he was. "Sure, you have that in common."

She traced the rim of her cold coffee cup, staring at her finger. "Sally is uncomfortable around me because I was inside her in my dream." She glanced up to see how Rory took that description. If he loved his boyfriend, he might not think she was wrong to have the ability to dream, to be a wraith.

"Sally is uncomfortable, period. She's been through a rough time." He paused. "She's probably most uncomfortable around Dad, to be honest."

Mala felt surprised. "Why would that be?" And how? Angus was just about the most comfortable person in the world to be around, though Rory might be a close second—he was certainly charming.

"Because he's the alpha, and that gives him a certain amount of power. That power unnerves Sally."

"I don't understand this alpha business," Mala admitted. "I mean I do in a way. He's in charge, he's the leader, people look to him. But at times people react more strongly to his position than I expect. As if he's some kind of...king."

"For what it's worth, Scott doesn't get the whole alpha thing either, so I wouldn't worry about it."

The door opened then, and the alpha himself stepped in, bringing cold air with him before he shut the door tight.

"Speak of the devil," murmured Rory.

"Were you?" asked Angus mildly as he divested himself of his outerwear.

"Singing your praises, Dad, that's all."

"Oh?"

"Yes, Mala was saying how people look up to you and she doesn't understand it."

"Well," began Mala, feeling that wasn't an accurate rendering of what she'd told Rory. "I don't understand everything about what being an alpha means."

At that Rory smirked at his dad and pulled on his own coat. "I'll leave you to explain everything." He turned back to her. "It was nice chatting with you, Mala. Good night."

"Good night," she said a little faintly. She'd been wanting him to leave, but she'd also meant to scoot upstairs so there wasn't an awkward good night with Angus. Eden had already left for her house down the road.

As Rory departed, another blast of cold air entered the restaurant, then Angus went and locked the door for the night. When he turned back, there was an intensity on his face she hadn't seen before. At least not when he focused on her.

"You doing okay? Rory treat you right?"

Of course Rory had treated her right. A more well-meaning and genial person she had yet to meet. "Yes."

"He should apologize for scaring you that other morning. But no doubt he's forgotten all about it."

She blinked as it took her a moment to associate Rory with the wolf that had followed her and frightened her during her first twenty-four hours in Wolf Town. "An apology isn't necessary. I'm just not used to seeing you as wolves. I haven't seen you as a wolf, for example."

He inclined his head in agreement, then took a seat beside her. He appeared to choose his next words with care. "It's true, you haven't. Would you like to see me as wolf?"

There seemed to be more to the question than she understood, rather like the alpha business, and she answered his question with a question. "Would you like me to dream of you, become part of you?"

"Before I had met you, no." He quirked his mouth. "I admit I'm curious now."

"I'm curious too. About you being wolf." She certainly wasn't curious about what it would be like to find him in her dream. That would be hell, given the usual state of wolves she was drawn to. She never wanted anyone, let alone Angus, so full of fear.

"I don't scare easily," he told her, tone quiet, and she thought of what Rory had said earlier, how her face was easy to read.

She couldn't meet his gaze. "I don't like the idea of you being threatened." It was the closest she could come to admitting she liked him. She didn't intend to give herself away. But she also couldn't hide her horror at the possibility of him being attacked.

He caught her face, gently, and smoothed a thumb across her cheekbone. She couldn't contain her shiver.

"If I had my way, you'd never have to dream again."

With his touch, she found she could look into his eyes. They were a warm blue and she wondered how she'd thought them cold when they'd first met. Intense, yes, but with a flame more than ice.

"That's not going to happen," she told him. "I gave up on the idea of my dreams stopping years ago."

"There was a time when I didn't want to turn wolf."

The thumb brushed her skin again, but this time she didn't care if her tremble gave her away. "I don't wish that on anyone, wanting to get rid of a part of you that is..."

"Essential?"

She shook her head, her cheek turning into his warm palm. When she made herself pull away, his palm slid down to rest against her neck.

"What then?" he asked, his voice mesmerizing.

"It's always felt like a burden, that's all." No, that wasn't quite right. So she amended, "It's always felt like a part of me too, but not essential, just...what I am and it's not going to change, not going to go away."

He kissed her cheek, and it felt like praise somehow. "If you wait another week, for the full moon, when it's easier for me to shift, I'll give you a demonstration, if you're still inclined. No pressure."

"Another week," she repeated. He didn't expect her to be gone in a week, and while she should have been dismayed, that wasn't the emotion she felt at all. She liked the idea of staying here with him, and his offering to show her his wolf felt like a gift. But he took her words differently and withdrew his hand.

"This isn't going to be over in a week, Mala." His strong arms crossed over his chest, muscles bunching as he gave a sympathetic shrug.

"I'm getting too comfortable in Wolf Town," she admitted.

"That's *really* not a problem."

She couldn't tell him she would be lonely when she went back, not when he was looking at her as if she meant something to him.

"I own a renovations company. What's your job?"

"Administrative assistant. I like it, when the people I work with are reasonable." She tried not to sound defensive. Her parents had expected more from her, but she'd had enough of school and had walked into this.

"I need an administrative assistant."

"Yeah, right."

"I couldn't be more serious."

It made her uneasy, this offer of work. "I'll be pushing someone out of their job, if there is one. If not, you don't need one."

"Wrong. Steve and Rory help me, but Steve would rather be doing the hands-on work and Rory has his accounting business to run. We're growing, as the town grows, so we need..." He smiled then, full blast, and it was both sweet and hot. "You."

She could feel the pulse going in her throat and she suddenly realized he could see it too. He could smell her, he'd said so more than once, and no doubt he understood she was increasingly attracted to him. She should have been mortified, but he took it all away by standing up to say, "Everything is going to be fine."

Chapter Sixteen

She'd been here before, of course she had—but quite a while ago. When she'd first left home, it had been a wild time sexually, mostly joyful, a few missteps. Nothing too deep either. Later she recognized she'd done that on purpose, wanting to avoid much actual sleeping together. That euphemism for sex was ironic, given her unique situation.

"Let's go upstairs," Angus said quietly.

Smiling at him, she wondered how he put her so at ease. She wanted to go to him, and in that unnerving way of his, he opened his arms.

She shook her head but rose. "I swear you guys are mind readers."

"Nah." He met her halfway and his warmth enveloped her, arms coming around her, head bending towards her.

"You just smell me and know everything." Her voice was muffled against his chest.

"And you smell wonderful."

She burrowed closer.

"I don't know everything, Mala." His chest rumbled against her as he spoke.

"Thank God."

With that, he slid a hand into her hair and pulled her face

from him so he was looking down at her, frowning a little. His other palm came up to cup her cheek. "Maybe you're too used to hiding."

Before she could protest, he brought his mouth to hers. "Shhhh," he whispered against her lips before he tasted her and she tasted him. It was leisurely at first, nice, comfortable, exactly what she wanted, her body softening under his, a wave of relief flowing through her. But then his muscles seemed to bunch beneath her hands, and he cradled her face and kissed her more deeply, stealing her breath. While she tried to catch up, she ended up clinging to him, holding on as he lifted her into his arms and she wrapped her legs around his hips.

He tamped down the kiss and nipped her bottom lip. "I don't want to trip on the steps."

She expected him to put her down, but he didn't, just strode up the stairs with her, though once they reached her door, something shifted between them, and he set her down.

He stroked hair off her face and she was reminded again how much she'd missed this. Whatever justification she'd created over these past years to accommodate her loneliness— that she was a cold adult who didn't need physical affection, that her youthful indiscretions could be ascribed to youth and rebellion... He'd demolished those ideas.

"Thinking so much," he said, voice low, and he seemed to be holding himself very carefully. "That can be our good-night kiss."

She lifted her chin and shook her head. "I'd rather sleep with you." She knew he wanted her, physically at least, and she couldn't see Angus kissing her if he had some other issue she wasn't aware of. He was very straightforward in his way.

He bent down to rest his forehead against hers. "I didn't mean this evening to go this way."

She searched for rejection in those words, but it wasn't there so she asked, "Why not?"

He kissed her eye, her cheek, her neck under her jawline where her pulse felt so strong and alive. "Because I've pretty much forced you to stay here, in Wolf Town. I feel it's on me to take extra care with how I treat you."

"Then it must be nice for you to understand that I want you. I know you know that."

He slid hands around her waist. "It is. More than nice." His voice deepened. "But I don't want you to feel manipulated later on."

Okay, some men had to be invited into your room, and Angus was one of them. She opened her door—she no longer bothered to lock it when she went out, the credit-card scare long past—and took his hand to lead him inside.

She was trembling a little, not from fear but anticipation. "I've shut down the last few years because of the dreams. I was scared this was over for me."

His eyes darkened. "Not if I have anything to do with it."

That hadn't come out quite the way he meant. He was trying not to come on too strong. He'd always been careful with his human lovers, restrained, and it was one more reason his life had been more celibate than not.

But she just grinned. He'd thought she'd be shy, so when her smile dimmed and a caution entered her expression, he was waiting for her to voice second thoughts. Instead, she asked, "Can we sleep together afterwards?"

He searched for the real meaning behind those words.

She traced a finger up the inside of his forearm, before she stepped back. "I think I can warn you that I sometimes scream in my sleep."

That touch of her finger had gone straight to his groin, but he attempted to process her words. "*I* think you're teasing me. A new side of you I haven't seen before."

She laughed, then bit her lip. "I've never had anyone accuse me of teasing them when I've warned them of my bad sleeping habits. In fact..."

But he didn't want her to be thinking of old lovers and, by the troubled expression on her face, what hadn't worked out. "Come here."

She raised one eyebrow. "Or what?"

He hadn't expected this playfulness. "Hmmm." He took a step towards her, watched her slide one foot backwards before he pounced, catching her up and hearing her squeal as she went up on his shoulder and then down on the bed, him right on top of her.

"So that's how you like it?" he asked.

She didn't bother to answer, just drew him in for another kiss as she arched to make full-body contact. This time, he meant to keep his head, but as her body softened under his, molding against him, he felt himself coming undone.

He pulled back, stroking her hair again, unable to completely detach.

She pushed up and him back. "Okay, Angus." When she nipped his neck, he groaned. "It's been three years for me. What's your timeline?"

He shook his head as she slid her slender hands under his shirt and pushed it up and off. The skin-on-skin contact was too much. He'd forgotten what he got like when he went too long.

"Keeping secrets?" She nuzzled his chest. "I'll have to pry

them out of you."

"No time for prying," he muttered and ripped open her shirt.

For a brief moment she looked surprised, and he stilled, but she laughed. "I think it's been a *little* while."

As he watched her undo his belt, he wondered at this alternating passive-aggressive approach of his. Not exactly Mr. Suave here. He cleared his throat.

She rose up on her knees and kissed him before he could speak, and he had enough time to think maybe they should talk afterwards, not now because he was too busy undressing her and tasting her mouth, her skin. Then he lifted her farther up to pull that beautiful dark nipple into his mouth.

She arched against him, making the most gorgeous sound, part moan, part sigh, like she'd been waiting forever for this moment. He laid her out on the bed and moved to her other breast, the areola and nipple primed just for him.

"God," she said, and he knew she was as ready as he was, that they'd been dancing around each other in their own way the entire time she'd been here, despite all the crazy goings-on, despite all her uncertainties. Sliding a hand down her soft belly, he came to curls, and she lifted her pelvis, encouraging him to explore farther. He teased that nub of hers that was already erect.

"Angus," she demanded, and he didn't know what the demand was, but entering her sheath with one finger set her off. She rippled under him as she cried out.

He kissed the underside of her breast and looked up, seeing her come down. An orgasm, though not a long one, and she wore a slightly sheepish expression, maybe even wary.

He smiled. "Well."

"I come fairly easily."

"I'll be sure not to take the credit."

The corner of her mouth curved up. "That's not what I meant."

As he slid another finger in her and cupped her mons with his palm, she sucked in a breath.

"I meant that I want you inside me."

"So that's what you coming means?"

That, or maybe his hand inside her, banished any wariness. "No. I just mean I like coming."

"Good." His cock, he'd been ignoring—or trying to—but her body and those words were making it painfully hard.

"Why aren't you undressed?"

In answer, Angus moved down in front of her. "Why not indeed?" He undid his zipper, but before going further, he leaned over to lap at her opening, tasting her juices then exploring her clit. He sucked it in his mouth, heard her slam the bed with her hand. With his thumb he rubbed against the bottom of her opening, collecting her come, then slid his thumb down to her nether hole and pushed in.

She cried out, much louder this time, her back rising, her body shaking as he sucked and stroked the sensitive skin below.

He didn't let her come down right away. Only once her body seemed to collapse did he kiss her clit goodbye and slide his thumb out.

She was flushed, her dark skin rich with blood, her full breasts proudly displaying erect brown nipples. As she lay there panting, he cupped her head and kissed her deeply. Receptive though not passive, she accepted him.

"I'll be right back." For good measure, he pulled a nipple

into his mouth and sucked hard twice, listening to her sigh as he released her, then padded off to the bathroom. Eden stocked the bathrooms with condoms, and he washed his hands while he was at it.

When he returned, she pushed herself up on shaky arms. Despite the tremor there, she insisted on taking off his jeans and briefs. And smiled at what she saw, his more-than-ready cock jutting out towards her.

"Hi, there," she murmured before caressing his balls and wrapping a hand around his erection.

"*I* am putting on the condom." His voice sounded almost guttural.

The look she gave him, beneath her lids, said she understood. "Okay."

As he ripped the packaging open and slid on the latex, he told her, "I'm glad you've waited for me. I'm feeling very possessive at the moment, I think I should warn you about that. But three years is too long."

She lay back, as if sitting up after his ministrations had taxed her, and simply opened her legs. It felt like the moment of truth as he climbed over her, positioned himself at her entrance.

"Over two years," he said.

She didn't smile then. She seemed to recognize it wasn't easy for him to admit that though she couldn't know why. Instead she slid her palm against his cheek and reached up for kiss. "Come inside me."

The latex wasn't his favorite way to make love, but with Mala he barely minded, she was so tight, her muscles hugging him close. He entered slowly and settled deep inside her, trying to savor the moment. If he was right, she'd come again, and at that point, it would be all over for him.

She molded up against him, consciously or not, seeking as much skin contact as possible. She was wolf-like in this, he thought dimly, or maybe it was just Mala herself. She moved when he didn't, encouraging him with her body and the noises coming from her throat. He didn't have it in him to explain he was trying to hold on.

"Christ," he said, letting go, forgetting about restraint. They were so close to the end it didn't matter if he lost it. He pulled out and pistoned in, gritting his teeth against the sensation that he was about to blow. *One more time.*

"One more time," she echoed, and he realized he'd said it aloud. "Harder," she encouraged, just how he wanted it, and he stroked into her hard and strong, reaching a rhythm right when she broke under him, a keening sound in her cry. His body seized and he slid home, emptying into the condom as her muscles pulsed around him, her arms and legs holding tight, like she didn't want to let him go.

He managed to keep his full weight off her, not crushing her into the soft bedding, while her body turned lax beneath his. She pressed kisses to his face.

Stroking his side, she made a soothing noise. He was trembling in the aftermath and she probably didn't know how to interpret that. As he softened inside her, he pulled out and stood beside the bed, taking care of the condom.

She protested, sliding a hand around his leg, and he nodded, unable to find words. He discarded the condom, returned to the bed and she curled into him. By the time he was ready to speak, she was fast asleep.

He had to smile, despite the shock of how their lovemaking had gone when he hadn't even been sure he should kiss her tonight. Quite simply he'd expected shyness and uncertainty, everything she'd shown him and the town over the week. He'd expected that she would need to be coaxed, that she would require a long road to seduction. Instead, she'd shed everything for him, no coyness, no hesitation—and very physical. His hunger had been matched by hers.

Rather like a wolf, he mused, and decided his stereotypes were long past their due date.

Also stereotypes about the sexes, because he was thinking she slept like a guy after sex. With that he closed his eyes and did the same.

Mala woke in what she thought was the middle of the night, only to see from a glance at the clock that it was early morning. Angus's arm lay across her stomach and she liked the warm weight of it. Like an anchor. She could imagine he'd kept the nightmares at bay, had allowed her to sleep deeply and calmly.

She shifted, trying to slide out from under his arm, and the lax muscles tensed, banded around her to hold her in place. He grunted softly against her shoulder but didn't wake. Instead of insisting, she lay still and drifted off to sleep again.

She floated down, and this time she stayed aware, recognized the horizon where beacons flared. Until recently she would have jolted awake or fallen into deeper sleep if she was exhausted. But for the first time she lingered, explored the potential of this dreamworld. She skimmed over this surface of mist. The tension within her ebbed as she could find no disturbance, could detect no one's presence. *It's peaceful*, she managed to think before easing into deeper sleep.

By the time Mala truly awoke, the bed was empty. Not cold, because she'd moved over to where Angus had slept and somehow kept all his warmth.

It was midmorning and Mala sat up, shocked at how long she'd slept. She'd thought that she'd already caught up on her sleep, but evidently not. Her bones felt relaxed, if that made any sense. Her body felt happy. Her mind, well, her mind wasn't sure. Morning-afters could be awkward.

She scrubbed her face, trying to waken more fully. If Angus would give her a bit of time to get herself together... She hadn't anticipated the sex, but she'd be okay. This usual tug-of-war within herself—the desire to cling, the desire to run away—neither option was viable, and perhaps more importantly, neither option was attractive. And she wanted to be attractive to Angus.

A shower would help her get hold of herself.

Before she dragged herself out of bed she burrowed into the sheets where he'd lain and pulled in a long breath, as if breathing him in, keeping their time together alive just a bit longer.

Well, she thought, as she stood up, muscles slightly sore in the most desirable way possible, Angus wanted her to stay. So it wasn't going to be her fault if she lingered in Wolf Town.

With a sharp nod to herself on that, she walked into the bathroom.

Chapter Seventeen

As planned, he traded off with Aileen at eight that morning. Anyone else might have acknowledged he was coming straight out of Mala's room, but not Aileen. She barely noticed. He'd once asked Jancis to have The Talk with Aileen, since the teacher claimed Aileen had slept through sex ed, and Jancis had shaken her head.

"Can't go there with her, Dad."

A piece of stone had lodged in his chest. "Trauma?"

Jancis had shrugged. "I don't even know."

But now Aileen simply said, "I'll stay here for the day." She shot him a smile. "I'm getting more and more used to this human thing. I don't think I've been human this often, ever."

"Why the change?"

"I like talking to Mala."

He searched for deeper meaning but couldn't find it. Though when Aileen watched over Sally, she tended to stay wolf, and stay outdoors.

"We're like sisters," she added, and while he liked hearing that, Angus wondered where Aileen got her idea of sisters from. She tipped her head towards the stairway. "Go on. I know you've got work to do."

He walked down those stairs, regretting there hadn't been

more sex or some cuddling in the morning. Mala had been sleeping deeply and he hadn't the heart to wake her when sleep was such a precious commodity to a wraith.

He would have woken if she'd had a nightmare or a terror. Though he didn't know how he'd feel about that—reluctant to rouse her in case she was seeing something important or saving someone, yet knowing she was frightened.

One thing at a time, he told himself as he headed home in the cold. She'd wanted him last night, and her directness had surprised him. He grinned, letting the physical memories wash over him. *Tonight*, he reminded his body that wanted more *now*. Today he had to work. But he'd phone Mala later and catch her voice on the line.

Tell her he was falling... He stopped himself on his front porch. Wolves sometimes moved too quickly for humans.

Nevertheless, he could tell her she was beautiful.

Once in the house, he exchanged good-mornings with Jancis and Caleb, then sat with Caleb for breakfast and walked him over to the school. It was a safety measure, though he didn't present it as such, and Caleb was still at the point where he was happy in Angus's company. Once Caleb was under Harrison's eye, Angus returned home and went to his landline for phone messages. These were the ones for the alpha, usually from out of town and often from the government.

He'd rather avoid government until after the Davies situation got resolved, so his finger hovered over the *Message* button. But avoidance wasn't a useful strategy when Davies might be around for days or weeks. God help him if it was months.

He jabbed the flashing circle.

"Hi, Angus?" He didn't recognize the female voice at first, and the intonation seemed off, like the speaker was stressed.

"It's Pamela. We met a little while ago. You came to my house asking about John? Well"—her voice caught—"I need your help. Call me." She gave out her ten-digit number haltingly.

In the background a male voice rumbled and the message cut out.

Angus shut his eyes. But the *Message* button continued to flash, and a second voice came on.

"Hi, Angus. It's Tony Rizzi from the Ministry of Public Safety. You didn't make our weekly conference call..." The words washed over Angus as he opened his eyes and stared at the phone talking to him. He liked Tony fine. He didn't like werewolves being slotted in to the Ministry of Public Safety but hadn't thought that a battle worth fighting. Yet.

"Call me back. Thanks!"

Angus wouldn't call Tony back. Not today. He pressed the heels of his hands against his eyes, then dialed Pamela's number.

She picked up on the third ring. "Hello?" she whispered, fear in her voice.

Not good.

He sat back and spoke as calmly as possible. "Pamela. Hi. It's Angus."

"Oh God." She let out a shaky breath, near tears.

He tensed in his chair and tried not to grip the phone too tight. "What's happened?"

"Come to 142 Pinetree Lane, North Bay. Alone. Now."

More rumbling and she seemed to be balking until she gave a short cry of pain and choked out, "If you don't do this in two hours, John's going to kill me."

"John, talk to me," he roared so the asshole could hear him through the line—to no avail. The dial tone was his only answer. He hit redial, but no one picked up so he threw the phone down on the table.

He had a sick feeling in his gut that after delivering her message to him Pamela was as good as dead, that Davies had no intention of letting her live now that she'd done what he needed of her—set the trap for Angus. Angus should never have called her back.

Fuck. He slammed his fist through the table and Jancis flew into the room.

"Dad?" she asked, her eyes growing wide.

He pulled his fist out of the particle board, shaking bits off his hand. Trying to regroup, he blew out a breath, hands now on his hips. The evening that he'd rung Pamela's doorbell and questioned her about Davies, he should have done more— warned Pamela to go into hiding, explained how dangerous Davies was. Never mind that she'd been convinced John had lost interest in her—Angus had bought into that. Once Davies discovered that Angus had talked to Pamela, she hadn't been safe.

"*Dad.*" This time a demand from Jancis who was getting in his face, insisting he pay attention to her. She wanted to help. "*What* is going on?"

He scrubbed his jaw, a part of him wishing his daughter need know nothing more, know nothing at all. But Jancis was capable and he required her assistance. "John Davies is luring me out of Wolf Town by threatening a woman's life. I believe he wants Caleb, Sally and Mala left unguarded."

"Since you're not falling for that, what's the catch?"

"He's going to kill that woman, and I can't sit by and let it happen."

"Dad," Jancis warned. "He may know you react to the damsel-in-distress scenario in this way. Don't let him manipulate you."

Damsel in distress. If he hadn't been so furious by the turn of events, he'd think harder on what his daughter meant. But he kept focused. "I have to try, Jancis. She, the woman, her name is Pamela..." He'd liked her well enough. She sure as hell didn't deserve this. "...was just talking to me. She's not dead yet. When I met her, she smelled honest, in a selfish way, but honest."

Jancis nodded once, accepting he was going to attempt to save Pamela. "Who are you taking with you?"

"He wants me to come alone." Which could mean Davies intended that Angus walk into a death trap.

"Right. So who are you taking with you?" Jancis said between gritted teeth.

"Rory. That'll leave most of the town here to be on guard. Phone everyone, get them on high alert. Phone Trey and let him know what's going on."

A shy expression flitted across his daughter's face, and Angus knew that her infatuation with Trey might never completely fade.

"I'm counting on you, Jancis."

She complied while Angus dialed his son. He hated that he was taking Rory into a dangerous situation. But he had no choice. This was his affable, generous, easygoing child, yes. However, Rory knew, better than anyone else in this town, how to kill.

Well, except for Angus himself.

"Two hours isn't a lot of time," Rory said mildly while he took apart and put together his Barrett in the backseat of the car. "And I don't want you going in alone."

Angus kept his eyes on the road and told his son, "I have you, with a sniper rifle."

"I'm not convinced that's the best strategy." An edge had entered Rory's voice. "Though if you're trying to protect me, it will accomplish that."

Angus gripped the steering wheel more tightly. "If you and I go in as wolves, they can pick us off, no problem. We'll be like sitting ducks."

"They can still pick *you* off."

"I'm sure Davies wants to talk to me," Angus argued. His gaze was drawn to the rearview mirror again. The silver car that had tailed them from five kilometers ago hadn't done a good job of hiding their intentions. As he took a sharp corner on to a county road, it followed.

"Excellent," deadpanned Rory. "That's the type of reassurance I like to hear. The psycho wants to talk to you before he kills you. You know he's already killed the woman—unless she's in on it."

"She's not in on it. I wish to God she were." Then he wouldn't have this guilt hanging around his neck like a millstone. It was going to slow him down if he wasn't careful.

In answer to that, Rory chambered a round.

"For God's sake, we have an hour to drive. What the hell are you doing that for?"

"I've been watching that car too, Dad. Clearly someone is following us and needs to be dissuaded."

Angus had planned to lose them, but they didn't have a lot of time, and Rory's choice was faster, if more risky. Rory opened the window to take aim behind them. Wolf reflexes were good, including those involved with guns, shooting and driving cars. And the county road was empty apart from the two of them.

Rory fired the shot, a tire blew and the vehicle careened off the road as it lost control.

His son pulled back in. "I think you should try that woman's number again, in case Davies wants to pick up the phone now and have a chat."

Once Angus hit Pamela's number—he'd put it in his cell before he left—he threw his phone into the backseat, and Rory caught it to listen to the phone ring.

After no one picked up, Rory dropped the phone beside him. "Great. No answer. How much backup do you think Davies has?"

"Honestly, not much." Angus trusted Trey's ability to ferret out information, and he'd made little headway with Davies. Rumors would have started if the number of wolves involved was more than a handful. "Or I wouldn't have dragged you into this."

Rory snorted in exasperation. "What would you have done? Gone in by yourself? Left this Pamela to their tender mercies?"

"I don't know," Angus said roughly. "I'm not dealing with what-ifs today."

"Uh-huh." Rory changed the subject. "Jancis says Trey wanted you to wait for him before you went after Davies."

Thing is, Angus would vastly prefer to go in with Trey than his son—and Trey knew it, knew Angus would choose the Rory-safe plan over the best possible plan if Rory was involved. The problem with waiting for Trey was that there was no time. It would take hours for Trey to arrive. If Angus was at all serious about trying to save Pamela, he had to be on the road now.

Not that he admitted all this to Rory, it would piss his son off. "Davies is a lone wolf," Angus argued. "He can't have many friends. You know that personality. We probably just got rid of half his recruits."

185

Rory grunted and Angus didn't push the argument further. He drove on, trying not to imagine Pamela and what he'd find of her at 142 Pinetree Lane.

"He had to go out of town," Aileen explained abruptly, as if Mala had been pestering her for information about Angus all morning and she was tired of repeating the same information.

Something about Aileen's delivery made Mala uneasy. There was a tension in Aileen's body that Mala didn't know how to interpret.

"Just like that?" Mala gave a shrug. "He...took off?"

Aileen stared at Mala before toying with the food on her plate. Aileen never toyed with food on her plate. She always ate full throttle. "A lot of demands are made on Angus. And he puts a lot of pressure on himself." Aileen gave herself a shake. "If he didn't, I'd still be roaming around northern Manitoba by myself."

"I'm glad he befriended you." Mala assumed that was how Angus had drawn Aileen to Wolf Town, although the face Aileen made had her wondering.

"He had to kidnap me first."

"Oh." Mala paused, suspicious of these sudden confidences. Aileen had been friendly, sure, but hadn't said much about herself until today. Mala put down her fork, losing her appetite. "Is Angus in some kind of trouble?"

"Why would you say that?" Aileen asked quickly.

"Because you're not eating your food."

Aileen's gaze jerked up and down, as if she'd been caught out. Then she grabbed her hamburger and took an enormous bite. In fact, she kept eating through her three-meals-in-one so that it was impossible for her to talk while Mala became increasingly dismayed. When Aileen wiped her mouth, she said, "He wouldn't sleep with you if he didn't like you."

Mala choked on her drink. "He told you that?" She sure as hell didn't want Angus talking to Aileen about them.

"He didn't have to." At Mala's nonresponse, Aileen added, "I could smell it."

"*Fantastic.*" But Mala paused again, suspicious of the intensity gripping Aileen. The girl was worried, and trying to keep Mala in the dark. Or perhaps Aileen didn't know how to cope. Mala leaned forward. "Aileen, tell me, is Angus in danger?"

A corner of Aileen's mouth turned down. "Maybe."

"John Davies?" Mala asked, and Aileen looked away.

Suddenly, Mala felt exhausted. Worrying about dream wolves and their fates had always taken their toll, even before she'd known they were real. But worrying about Angus overwhelmed her, especially the thought that he might be up against the man who had terrorized people.

In her dreams.

She'd battled Davies in her dreams before—and won. There weren't all that many things she was skilled at, but this dream-wraith thing, well, she'd accomplished something with that.

Mala made a decision. It might be difficult, it might be impossible to self-direct when the situation affected her so strongly and so personally. It might be impossible to discover or even identify Angus's beacon.

Nevertheless, she was going to attempt to find Angus on that horizon where beacons flared.

Angus's wolf allowed him to put down his guard and forsake his protective instincts enough for him to walk away, leaving Rory by himself, to scout out this location on Pinetree. His son was safely hidden, a rifle to defend himself, and Angus hadn't been able to detect any wolves or people lurking in the woods behind the house where Rory stayed out of sight. Now to determine if there were people in the house or beyond it, towards the road. While a part of him wanted to rush this encounter then get back to Rory and ensure his safety, Angus approached the house with care.

Because getting himself shot, for example, wouldn't help Rory at all.

Whether Davies expected Angus to stroll up as human and knock on the door or not, he didn't know, but Angus decided against it. He wanted to fully use his wolf senses during this rendezvous.

The wind was blowing, the lightest swirling of snow in the air and a thick white layer covered the ground. Under the circumstances, it would have been better if he were a white wolf, though they were rare among weres. His gray fur remained visible so he carefully observed the house, trying to pick up sounds and smells.

The smell of death came to him first and drew him closer. And while there were the scents of those who had been here, both werewolf and human, and they were fresh, the house was silent. Despite the danger of being upwind from the road, Angus felt compelled to identify who had died and the silence called to him. He pulled in a breath, closed his eyes, and leapt through the basement window at the side of the house. Glass shattered around him but his thick coat prevented him from being cut, and he landed effortlessly on the cement basement floor.

Not much finesse, this break-in, and he preferred to be less obvious during an investigation, but Rory was alive out there and someone was dead in here, so Angus needed answers fast.

It didn't take long to find her. He climbed the stairs from the basement and took a right into the kitchen. There was no subtlety in this act. They'd gutted Pamela, left her to bleed out in a painful death, her life's blood puddled on the linoleum as she curled around herself, a hand over her sliced-open belly, perhaps trying to put herself back together.

Angus forced himself to observe her body and make sure it was Pamela, make sure he understood exactly how these men had chosen to kill her.

Make sure he'd have no qualms in killing these men in turn.

As to when she'd been murdered? He'd guess as soon as they'd hung up on him, over two hours ago, when they'd decided she was no longer any use to them. The smell of death had accumulated in this room.

She didn't deserve this fate, her curled-up body on a dirty kitchen floor. Angus wanted to mete out justice, here and now. He lifted his head, trying to clear it from the rage that rolled over him in a wave of fury.

Rory. He remembered his son then—human and alone. The fur on the back of Angus's neck rose. He didn't like Rory to be in the forest, albeit armed, when these monsters had recently killed. Angus shot out of the room, down to the basement and back through the broken, jagged window.

It was as he regained his footing outside the house that something heavy smashed down on his hindquarters. Through the pain of breaking bone, he swung his body round, snarling, ready to attack. He refused to go down like this.

But movement from the corner of his eye was his only warning before pain collided with his skull, and his world disappeared into blackness.

Chapter Eighteen

"I want you to understand something." The words came at Angus as if from far away, yet also as if from inside an echo chamber. They blurred together and faded out. Blackness swept over Angus and he knew nothing.

He came back to the world, and the words returned, similar and different. This time a face went in and out of focus, as well, a mouth moving out of sync with the noises it made.

Eventually the words coalesced to say— "I am John Davies."

Angus's head hurt, and he knew the situation was bad, but he couldn't yet recall the specific reasons why. He tried to blink and realized he was in wolf form, felt his wolf's brow furrow. He needed to shift, he'd been wounded and required healing. But he couldn't shift if it wasn't safe to do so.

Enemy, his muzzy brain told him, and that sharpened his thinking.

"You've interfered," Davies continued, his words and then his face becoming clearer for a moment. "Look at me. I want you to see who you've been fucking with. Your latest sin was to shoot out the wheel of my men's car. You don't get to do that without being punished."

Angus breathed in, letting the voice wash over him. His internal clock said he'd been passing in and out of consciousness for over half an hour. He tried to take stock of his situation. They were on the road, in a van, moving forward. The twists and turns suggested a side road, not a highway.

There was another man in the van, the driver. He was non-wolf and easy to dispose of if it came to that. Angus turned his aching head back to Davies and found himself looking at a middle-aged werewolf with gold-brown eyes and a thick beard.

"You're in a cage, Angus," Davies informed him.

That explained the metal bars surrounding him. They hadn't registered past the throbbing in his skull.

And then he remembered: *Rory*. Had they got him? Was he dead?

Some of the new tension in his body must have alerted Davies because he drawled, "Back in the land of the living, MacIntyre? Fully awake? I should warn you, it won't be for long. We're just going to the right secluded place so your pack spends precious resources trying, and failing, to find you. But not to worry, we're mostly on our way to Wolf Town, where I have my son and girlfriend to pick up. You may have met them, Caleb and Sally."

Davies hadn't mentioned Rory. He'd rub it in Angus's face if he'd gotten his hands on Rory.

"I also," he added softly, "want to pick up the new girl in town, a certain Mala. I hear she's *special*."

He turned a gun this way and that in his right hand, making clear his plans for Mala. Once he tired of listening to the sound of his own voice, Davies was going to shoot Angus in the head and go on to harm the people he cared for.

This was unacceptable.

"Do you know how I know Mala is fucking special?" Davies raised one eyebrow in question. "Because she's been *inside* me.

191

I can't decide if I should kill her for that or try to use her abilities in some way. Thing is, I'm pretty sure that'll be too complicated and I don't like complicated. I need Mala dead, don't I?"

Angus gave up staying quiet. He couldn't restrain himself, and his wolf raged. So he roared, ignoring his pain and his useless lower half, and leapt with all his forelegs' strength against the bars. They creaked but did not give, and it took everything in him not to pass out as he fell to the ground.

Davies laughed, pleased. "You like her, do you? I could try—"

The shot came out of nowhere, shocking Angus back to clear thinking. It hadn't been Davies's gun that fired though, but one from outside. The van skidded and shook with a tire gone flat.

Rory's modus operandi.

The driver swore in alarm while brakes squealed, slowing them to a crawl. At which point a second shot took out the driver himself. Davies made as if to shoot at Angus, but before he could aim the pistol properly, the van hurtled downwards and sideways, and Davies lost his position, was thrown against the side window.

The van crashed, overturning, the cage with it. The abrupt stop caused Angus's body to be flung against the bars of the cage, and pain seared through him. Pure willpower kept him conscious. It took Angus a moment of silence to understand that the impact had thrown the cage on top of Davies, who lay trapped beneath it.

Angus pushed his pain away, refused to go under at this critical juncture. Instead he tore at the human skin that pressed against the bars, searching for a vulnerable artery, and found one in the arm. When his teeth snagged on the forearm,

192

he bit Davies as deeply as possible. Blood spurted, pouring out of the wound.

Angus tried to find another way to harm his captor, but Davies was fighting for his life, struggling to find his way out from under Angus. Agony ripped through Angus again, and this time his vision started to fade. He barely managed to observe Davies as he crawled out from beneath the cage then tore a piece of cloth off his own shirt and tried to bind his wound before he bled out. The artery was pumping.

Davies wasn't going to shift when under attack. As he wrapped the makeshift bandage, the blood flowing out of his arm slowed. He gritted his teeth and wrapped it tighter. Suddenly, he turned his focus elsewhere, jerking his head up, and through his pain, Angus tried to figure out why. He watched Davies reach over to where his pistol had been thrown, pick it up and fire straight out the side window.

The bullet went through the glass and came right back, powering directly into Davies's chest. Blood bloomed like a dangerously red flower opening up in the man's breast.

Angus's sluggish thoughts pieced together that the bullet hadn't actually come back, that someone else had shot Davies dead. He fiercely held on to consciousness, trying to think things through, trying to identify his next course of action.

Then the back door of the van was flung open and Rory dragged himself inside, one hand holding his rifle, the other clamped on his shoulder, blood seeping through his fingers.

Rory yanked the van door shut. "I hope to hell that's it, Dad, because I've got no choice."

The rifle clattered on the van floor and Angus had enough wherewithal to realize Rory had no choice but to shift to wolf to heal.

Angus had to guard his son.

He was badly wounded and caught in a fucking cage.

The rage threatened to overwhelm him and his vision grayed. Between the pain and the rage, he was going crazy. He was going under.

Angus?

He growled, searching, unable to focus on what he was searching for. His son's body had slowed the bleeding, the first step in Rory's transformation from human to wolf. A relief to see that, even if the idea of Rory being wounded assailed Angus, panicking him.

Oh, Angus. The sadness inside him was puzzling. And this wasn't how he addressed himself.

"Where are you?"

It was then he felt a...presence. Like a part of him, but separate. Feminine.

His first instinct was to conclude he was hallucinating. He was in too much pain, his pelvis shattered, some brain damage from the blow to his head. He needed to shift and soon, repair himself before any of the damage became permanent.

"Then, my God, Angus, shift. Don't wait any longer." She sounded alarmed, and her presence became suddenly and overwhelmingly familiar.

He couldn't believe it and he utterly did believe it. *"Mala?"*

"Yes. It's me."

He didn't recognize her exactly—how could you recognize someone inside yourself?—but he knew it was her and with that knowledge came relief.

"Angus," she thought at him. *"You must tell me where you are. So we can help you."*

"I can't. I don't know. Rory, Rory will know." The wound was clotting, as Rory's human body began to recede. *"But I have to*

protect him.*"

"I'm going to look out through your eyes. Okay?"

He closed his eyes briefly, not because he didn't want her to see, but because the sensation of her becoming a part of him relaxed him.

"It's not just my presence." Her voice inside him sounded wry. *"I'm taking away some of your pain. I know how to draw away emotions. I don't know if I ever explained that to you."*

He supposed that was good. It sounded good. If incomprehensible. Something to think on later.

"Yes, think about it later. But it is good," she assured him. *"Thank you for welcoming me, Angus. I've never been welcomed before. Of course, it would be easier to appreciate if you weren't in such pain."*

He didn't like it either. And then he remembered this was their morning-after reunion. The strangest morning-after he could ever remember.

"Mine too," she thought grimly. She seemed to be working, his perception was sensation and feeling, nothing he could see. But when he looked inward, he was able to perceive she was gathering something.

"This is your pain," she explained. *"It's too much for you to bear alone. It is harming you."*

"Don't you take it on, Mala," he warned. He didn't want it in her, didn't want her to carry it.

"That's not how it works. It doesn't hurt me at all."

"It's mine," he insisted.

"Yes," she agreed. *"But I can use it, you see, to harm others."* He could feel her cringe at this admission and decided now was not the time to argue or discuss this.

"We'll talk about that later too," he told her, and felt her

195

smile.

Then something changed, abruptly, and she grew still within him, the sense of a smile vanishing, and a tension radiated out from her. *"Look out, Angus."* Barely able to hold on, he hadn't been looking out at all. She had been seeing for him. *"There is more than one wolf shifting in the van with you. More than Rory. Look at John Davies."*

Angus forced himself to focus, to process what he observed—Davies beginning to heal. The injury to his chest, while severe, had the potential to close.

She'd gone quiet and he didn't know what it meant.

"Mala?" he asked.

"Don't you worry about me, Angus," she said, and he feared what she was going to do next. *"I promise you I'm safe, and I will see you again."*

"Mala!" he yelled inwardly, but it was too late. She was gone, and with her absence, there came a mental flash, something powerful and bright ghosting through his mind's eye and leaving him empty. He had the impression of sharp brightness being aimed towards the man who was trying to survive by shifting from man to wolf.

He watched, but could not see an outward difference in Davies who had been silent and still before Mala had attacked him and remained silent and still afterwards. Movement in the corner of his eye caused him to turn his head.

"Dad?" said Rory groggily. Somehow, Rory had managed to half-shift and shift back to human, healing enough that he could get by. A good trick they'd practiced from time to time but, till now, had never chosen to use. Rory reached up and undid the lock on Angus's cage, and Angus wanted to yell at him too. Instead he growled while he looked at Davies.

Rory turned, but all he saw was a dead man, and he pulled

a face of disgust at the sight. "The world's better off without him." He opened the door to Angus's cage. "Dad, you've got to shift. I can guard you. I'm healthy and I'm armed."

Rory patted the rifle for good measure. Despite everything that had gone on, or because of it, it was time to shift to human. Angus wanted to walk out of the godawful cage first, but he couldn't. He couldn't move.

There were signals, long established, and Angus used them. Though it was difficult, he lifted his right paw, to Rory's consternation, and gave it a slight seesaw motion, asking Rory to tell him where they were.

"Jesus, Dad, quit hurting yourself. I don't know exactly, it doesn't really matter, but we're on Red Hawk Lake. I think that asshole was planning to drown you or something." Rory brought his hand to Angus's head, making contact, encouraging Angus's body to move to its human form. "I'll guard you. Now, shift."

There was no way Angus could communicate to Rory that Mala had been here, had gone over to Davies to complete the werewolf's death. Angus glanced over at the dead body one more time and, as if from a great distance, he heard her words, her thoughts.

"Shift, Angus, shift."

Then: *"I promise I will see you soon."*

And Angus took her word for it, relaxed as far as he was able, and called to his human.

He first became aware of cold metal under his cheek. Odd. His shoulder, too, lay on metal. His torso hurt like hell, but he could move. He blinked rapidly—always an indication he was human, in case the bare skin wasn't indicator enough—and became deeply confused. What the fuck was he doing naked in a cage in the fucking winter?

197

"Next time you come up with a plan, you don't protect me." Rory's voice was rough with anger.

Angus turned his head to meet Rory's hard gaze and tried to remember what they were doing and why his son was furious. He went to pull himself forward.

And failed, pain and weakness overwhelming him. "What the hell?"

"Don't move," Rory commanded. "Those bones of yours have been shattered for more than an hour. They're barely knitting themselves together despite the shift."

"Ah, fuck." It all came back then. Pamela, they'd gone to rescue her and it had been a futile endeavor, a trap. She was dead; it hurt to remember that.

Angus was supposed to be dead too, but his clever son had prevented this and Davies... Angus remembered the man had been trying to shift. He glanced into the corner of the upended van and the body was gone.

"I threw him in the lake," said Rory.

"Was he dead?"

Rory stared back at him in disbelief. But he, like any werewolf, understood the fear of wolves resurrecting themselves. Their bodies were more resourceful than most people could ever predict. "He sure as hell was. But if he survived my bullet, he won't survive in freezing water."

"The other body?" Angus recalled there'd been a driver.

"I'll leave him for someone to find, on the chance he has family who'd be worried about him."

"We have to scrub ourselves off this van. I can't be explaining our blood to the provincial government."

"I know. I called home. A team is coming to get us and clean up."

"Mala." He hoped to hell she hadn't gone into the freezing water with Davies. He hoped she was awake.

Rory cocked his head. "Mala? She's safe."

"She was here. She killed Davies." Had she ever killed anyone before?

His son looked dubious then started glowering again, and Angus braced himself for a lecture.

"Don't you ever come up with such a shitty plan that puts *you* in all the danger and keeps me safe."

"You're the one who took a bullet to the shoulder and almost died."

"Bull. Shit. I was nowhere near death. And Davies could have just as likely killed you as not."

"Well, he didn't, did he?" Unfortunately those last words came out through chattering teeth. Between the cold temperatures and his injuries, his shift's heat production had flared and died more quickly than usual.

"Don't move." Rory pointed a finger at him. He jumped out of the van and returned with a blanket from their car. He gently wrapped it around Angus, protecting him from the worst of the cold.

"What are we waiting for? Let's go home."

"We're waiting for Teo who's..." Rory checked his watch, "...twenty minutes out. He's coming with a stretcher and an ambulance. If I carry you to the car, I'm going to break your pelvis again. And then I'll have to answer to Teo, which I have no desire to do."

Angus considered protesting—they were leaving themselves vulnerable if a stranger came upon them. Except this was an out-of-the-way spot and he couldn't face a second broken pelvis in one day.

Rory's expression softened. "Yeah, you'll listen to me for once and we'll wait."

"Is Mala coming?"

For the first time that day, something like amusement crossed Rory's face. "As a matter of fact, she is. Apparently Teo and Aileen could not convince her to stay back. They would have had to peel her off the side of the ambulance."

Angus smiled at the image.

Rory raised one eyebrow. "Is there something you want to tell me about you two, Dad?"

But Angus was too exhausted for explanations so he just said, "Not right now."

Epilogue

Angus sat down to help Caleb with algebra. "You have some aptitude when it comes to math."

Caleb snorted and hunched over his work but he smelled...pleased. "I don't hate it anymore."

"That's progress."

The boy had filled out in the last two months. He was growing taller and broader, now that the shadow of his father had disappeared. Angus had wondered if Caleb would have mixed feelings about his father's death—and who had caused it—but there were none. There had been no bond between father and son, only fear and hate.

His mother, Shanna, was back in Caleb's life though. They'd agreed to keep her son here, but she'd visited, and Caleb would be going to Chicago for the major holidays and part of the summer vacation. With Davies gone, Caleb and Shanna could build back up their relationship.

Sally was another matter. She remained thin and withdrawn, close to friendless despite her being polite to everyone except Mala. The fact Sally didn't want to leave Wolf Town had to be the extent of her progress for the moment. Though he'd arranged for Veronica to visit because the two had struck up an email friendship.

And then there was Mala. The one non-wolf, not even wolf-related if the blood test was a true indication. There was a lot to learn about her, she had a lot to learn about herself, and yet, it was as if she'd always belonged here in Wolf Town. With Angus. Accepted by others. If nothing else, taking part in killing Davies had won Mala points with a lot of people.

"Angus?"

He pushed out all thoughts but those focused on Caleb and pointed out an arithmetic mistake.

Then he went stock-still. Caleb glanced at him, concerned at the change in his demeanor. "You okay?"

It had taken a few weeks for Angus to recover from Davies's assault and ever since then, any twinge got Caleb worried.

"It's not that," Angus assured Caleb. "It's..."

"Hi, Angus." She sounded shy. This was the second time Mala had succeeded in finding him in her dreams when life was normal and he was down the hall. In her dreamworld it was apparently difficult to locate people who weren't distressed. But he was distinct to her and she was learning to identify his marker.

Whatever that was. She hadn't been able to describe what she experienced in any but the most abstract of ways. Describing the process as akin to playing hide the thimble didn't do much to increase Angus's understanding.

"It's what?" Caleb asked.

It felt odd, too private, to admit Mala was inside him. But they'd gone for transparency when it came to her abilities, in order to reassure the denizens of Wolf Town that she wouldn't be entering them willy-nilly and without permission.

"Mala."

Caleb's eyes widened. Although given his past experience and how she'd saved him, he was one of those least disturbed by what Mala could accomplish.

"Excuse me, okay?"

Caleb nodded and Angus ruffled his hair before walking down the hall to the bedroom.

"You okay?" he asked her.

"Yes, but I can't last long. You're too happy, too calm, too well-adjusted."

He grinned. *"I sound fantastic."*

That shyness returned. *"You are to me."*

Angus softly opened the door to see Mala sleeping in their bed, one hand tucked under her cheek. *"Do you see what I see?"*

Just like that she was gone from him, leaving an empty space inside. Her eyes flew open and, clearly disoriented, she stared at him standing in the doorway.

"Shhh," he said, going to her while she pushed up to sitting. She still seemed confused, so he gathered her up against him, nuzzling her neck.

"Why do you do that?" she demanded, voice thick with sleep. "I'm practicing, like I'm supposed to, and you push me out."

"I didn't push you out."

"I freaked out when I saw myself. I told you that would happen."

Angus felt a little sheepish. He'd have to do better next time, have more faith in her. "I worry if you're okay when you're not wholly in yourself."

She sat up straighter, wrapped her arms around his neck and kissed him, opening herself to him so they could leisurely explore each other's mouths. He sank one hand into her hair and curled another around her soft, warm hip.

Then she pulled away. "*You* worry." She shook her head. "You're one to talk. I haven't recovered from finding you in such pain in that upturned van. I brace myself *every single time* I find you. It's one of the hardest things I do."

At her shiver, he ran a hand up and down her back. She'd been more traumatized by that event than him. She'd been with hurt, even dying, wolves before. But no one she'd known in real life and certainly not her lover. Only later had Teo described how frantic Mala had been that day.

In truth, Angus feared for what the future would bring Mala, when the nightmares returned to her one day. She took it hard, understanding the truth about her dreams—that they were real.

As if reading his mind, she declared, "I can handle it. Knowing I can truly help, it makes a difference."

At least with Davies dead and no known sociopathic wolves on the loose, it might be a while. She deserved that respite. "You're right, you can. I believe in you." He sighed, breathing in her scent. "Even if I'd like to be able to do it for you."

She mouthed his neck. "You like to do too much for too many people. For better or worse, this is my gift." Then she added more softly, "And I'm grateful you let me practice on you."

He slipped a hand under her shirt. He'd been alone, sexually, for so long that he treasured every moment they could touch. And though she was human, she welcomed him fully.

She went up on her knees so she was above him, and looked him straight in the eye. "Angus?"

He traced a finger up her spine. "Yes?"

"You're the first one who is glad to have me...visit. Ever."

He simply smiled.

"It's kind of wonderful for me."

He rested both palms at her waist. "Don't doubt how much I want you, Mala." He could tell how much she wanted him, he didn't have reason to entertain any doubts. But she managed to fill herself with insecurities and fears. Her years on her own had done damage to her self-confidence.

"But that's what I'm saying. When I was with you just now, you were happy to see me." Her eyes got shiny. His Mala didn't really cry, he'd learned that in their two months together, but she allowed herself this small sheen of tears.

"Of course I was," he said quietly before cradling her face and kissing both her eyes. "I love you and I'll always be happy to see you."

She bit her lip, taking in his statement, and broke out in a smile. He could only describe her as radiant as she reached for him and buried her face in his neck, right where she belonged.

About the Author

Jorrie Spencer has written for more years than she can remember. Her latest writing passion is romance and shapeshifters. She lives with her husband and two children in Canada.

To learn more about Jorrie Spencer please visit www.jorriespencer.com or send an email to Jorrie Spencer at jorriespencer@gmail.com.

She also writes as Joely Skye (www.joelyskye.com).

PUBLISHING

www.samhainpublishing.com

Green for the planet.
Great for your wallet.

It's all about the story...

Romance

HORROR

www.samhainpublishing.com

CPSIA information can be obtained at www.ICGtesting.com
Printed in the USA
BVOW011250140312

285173BV00002B/3/P